Fate Comes Softly

by

Loretta C. Rogers

A Wild Rose Press Bouquet

This is a work of fiction. Names, characters, places, and incidents are either the product of the author's imagination or are used fictitiously, and any resemblance to actual persons living or dead, business establishments, events, or locales, is entirely coincidental.

Fate Comes Softly

COPYRIGHT © 2018 by Loretta C. Rogers

Cover Art by *Lisa Dawn MacDonald*

The Wild Rose Press, Inc.
PO Box 708
Adams Basin, NY 14410-0708
Visit us at www.thewildrosepress.com

Publishing History
First Cactus Edition, 2018
Print ISBN 978-1-5092-2148-6
Digital ISBN 978-1-5092-2317-6

A Wild Rose Press Bouquet
Published in the United States of America

Saving Liberty

by

Loretta C. Rogers

Dedication

Saving Liberty
Is dedicated to
women who have survived abuse and can still smile.

Chapter One

Ethan Wheeler ran bloodied hands down the sides of his pants. With the deer carcass secured to the pack mule, he decided to wash away the saccharine metallic odor of blood before returning to his homestead. Always alert for hostiles, he stepped quietly through the forest to a nearby stream. A feeling of unease settled over him. Only the sound of a spring breeze disturbed the silence. Not even the birds twittered.

For a moment, he thought his mind played tricks on him. He shook his head in denial. What the hell was a woman doing this far from civilization, and why was she kneeling at the edge of the creek—praying? And then he saw it—the thick-bodied moccasin coiled at the hem of her skirt. What he saw wasn't a figment of his imagination.

He grimaced at the hard knot that tightened his gut. How long could she remain on her knees with her hands pressed together before her legs numbed and the muscles in her thighs objected to the strained position? He swallowed the dryness that hovered unwelcomed in his throat, and did his own praying as he eased the rifle to his shoulder, sighted down the barrel, and then decided not to shoot. He couldn't risk missing the snake and hitting the woman.

With the greatest of care, he lowered the weapon and leaned it against a tree. He reached for the skinning knife and slid it from the scabbard at his waist. No matter how much strength he put into the toss, the distance was too great for the blade to hit its mark.

He stepped lightly, one foot at a time. He picked up the next, testing his ability to tread silently. He needed to get close enough to make his lob as deadly as the viper's bite. Time was of the essence. He was certain the woman's legs were screaming in torment by now and that any moment she would collapse and bring about her own demise.

In the cold April dusk, sweat pooled beneath Ethan's doeskin shirt as he drew back his arm and concentrated on his aim. As he edged forward, the inevitable happened. He stepped on a twig. The loud snap caused the girl to jerk in his direction.

She cried out and grabbed her wrist.

Water splashed high, raining down droplets as Ethan dashed across the shallow stream. Before the moccasin could strike again and milk its poison into the young woman, he grabbed it behind the head; the dark banded body coiled around his arm. The venomous mouth opened wide to expose lethal fangs. Its hooded elliptical eyes, as evil as any devil's, seemed to exude malice.

With one slice of the blade, Ethan separated the head from the body and flung both away. He lifted the girl into his arms and carried her up the slope.

She moaned as she laid her head against his chest. "My baby. Please don't let my baby die."

Ethan darted a quick glance around for the child as he knelt to prop the woman against a tree. He ripped the sleeve of her dress to the shoulder. "I'll look for your baby as soon as I tend this bite."

He rushed back to the stream to rinse the blade and then dried it against his pants leg as he returned to the girl. "This may hurt. I need to make a cut so I can suck out as much venom as possible. Do you understand?"

Her eyes remained closed. He gently nudged her shoulder. "Ma'am?"

She nodded her understanding, her voice a weak sigh. "My ba...by..."

It seemed life left her body, and her head lolled to one side.

Ethan leaned close and was relieved when he felt a whisper of breath against his cheek. "Stay strong...think good thoughts. As soon as I get the poison out, I'll look for your baby. Keep thinking about your child." He continued to talk. "Children shouldn't grow up without a mother's love."

He thought about his motherless son and allowed a swift second of nostalgia to drift over him. Rallying, and with a swift motion, he used the tip of his knife to cut an X in the soft flesh between her elbow and wrist, thankful the moccasin had missed the girl's pulse. He lifted her arm and placed his lips over the area.

She moaned again.

He drew deep, filling his mouth with salty, acidic fluid. He spat, careful not to swallow, then repeated the process until satisfied that he'd extracted as much venom as possible.

When finished, he lifted the hem of her dress and used the knife to cut two strips of cloth from the white under-slip.

Though her eyes remained closed, and her breathing was shallow, he touched her shoulder. "I have to leave you for a moment."

Her lips moved, the words almost inaudible. "Am I going to die?"

"No, ma'am, not if I can help it. Sorry about ruining your undergarment. I need a wet cloth to cleanse the wound, and another to bind it, and I must get my horse, which is on the other side of the creek."

One thing for certain, he didn't have the skills to give her better medical attention. Not that there was a doctor within two hundred miles of Goss Point, Missouri. The least he could do was provide her with a soft bed, nourishment, and comfort until she lived or…a breath hitched painfully in his throat…until he added another cross in his small graveyard, on a knoll under a sweet gum tree overlooking his homestead.

"I'll be right back, ma'am." He laid a reassuring pat on her shoulder.

He hastened to the edge of the stream, where he knelt and filled his cupped hands with water. He swished the cool liquid inside his mouth and spat it out. As much as he desired to drink, he gargled, then swooshed and spit three more times to cleanse his mouth. After dampening the strip of cloth, he tucked it inside his waistband. In two long strides, he sprinted to the opposite bank, where his dun gelding and the pack mule remained tethered.

A new dilemma assailed him. Fresh meat was essential to replenish his empty smokehouse, but the mule was cantankerous and slow and would make traveling difficult. Yet if he left the mule to find its own way home, the venison might rot. Ethan gave himself a swift mental kick. He could hunt another day. The young woman's life was more important.

Picking up a long, thin branch, Ethan pointed it

toward the short-legged jack. The animal rolled the whites of its brown eyes toward the man's voice. "Listen, Stubborn. Today isn't the day to plant your feet and live up to your name. You don't want to be the reason a young woman dies, do you?"

The gray mule flicked its lopped ears back and forth as if understanding each word. The animal pawed the ground, lifted its short thick head, and stared with obstinate eyes. Ethan said, "You're not gonna like this, but if it'll light a fire under you, so be it." Ethan drew back and laid a stinging blow across the mule's rump. The animal loosed a loud bray, kicked its heels, and lit out in a bucking gallop.

Grabbing the reins of his gelding, Ethan leapt into the saddle and splashed across the creek. His voice grim, he spoke only to the wind. "At least Stubborn is headed in the direction of home."

Leaving the horse ground-tied, Ethan knelt beside the girl and gently lifted her swollen arm. He used the moist cloth to wipe away the blood and a small dribble of yellow venom. When he spoke, his voice was quiet and calm. "Ma'am, what are you doing out here all alone?"

She looked at him with an expression of overwhelming sadness. "They left me."

The crystalline blue of her eyes drew him like a pond would draw a man dying of thirst. "Who?"

Tears leaked down her cheeks. "The wagon train."

A slow frown covered Ethan's face as he rolled back on his knees. He'd come west on a wagon train and knew the wagon master's word was law. There were only two reasons for banishing a member from the group—infection with a deadly disease or commitment of an unpardonable sin. Crimes like theft and murder were punishable by hanging.

He studied the woman's face and bare arm. No sign of smallpox or typhus was evident. Ethan drew a deep breath and gave himself a moment. Surprise rocked him. He wanted to know the secrets of this slip of a girl whose golden hair reminded him of a sheaf of wheat. What transgression had she committed that was so vile that it justified being abandoned in the middle of no-man's land with only a baby?

"I don't understand. Are you infected with a disease?"

He used the second strip of cloth to bind the wound. The dark bruising under her eyes told him he needed to hurry.

She coughed, then retched. "My arm hurts."

"Yes ma'am, but are you—"

"I'm terrified." Her voice was hushed and jerky.

He tore another strip from her chemise and used it to wipe her mouth. It was obvious the effects of the poison were wending their way through her body. Emotions warred inside him—take time to look for the baby or get the woman to his home? Another concern filtered through him. If this woman was diseased, he risked infecting his son. He was furious with himself and with her for putting him in this position.

Her eyes fluttered open. The smile on her face trembled, then crumpled. "What is your name, gallant sir?"

"Ethan Wheeler, ma'am."

She reached up to touch his face. As if the effort was too much, her hand dropped to her lap. Before she fainted, she whispered, "Bad man."

"No, ma'am. You have my word that I'll bring no harm to you."

Again her eyes opened. "Not you...him." Her eyelids closed as her voice faded.

"Does this man have a name?"

She didn't answer.

He patted her cheek. "What about you—how are you called?"

She rallied for a moment. "I'm..." It seemed the effort to speak exhausted her.

Ethan wondered who the *bad man* was as he leaned forward to check her breathing. Satisfied that he'd done all he could without adequate medical supplies, he left the unconscious woman.

Frantic to find the child before wolves or other predators did, he explored the immediate area. Walking a close perimeter to the creek, he used his scouting skills to look for signs of where the child might have crawled away.

Nothing.

Widening the borders of his search, he spotted a large brown object about fifty yards in the distance and sprinted toward it. A steamer trunk. He unbuckled the straps to find it filled with an assortment of clothing and books. It struck him as odd that no baby clothes were in the trunk.

Still, the woman had been adamant about the child. He lifted on his knees and spotted the trail of drag marks and wondered who had pulled the heavy chest to this point. Surely not the frail woman? He followed the trace for a goodly distance.

Still no baby.

Distress clawed his gut. It took stamina and

fortitude to survive the wilderness. Even the strongest of men broke their backs and died trying to conquer an unforgiving land. An infant hadn't a prayer of a chance.

He turned in a slow but complete circle. Where was the child? No torn remnants of clothing or blood to suggest an animal had carried it away—or worse, fed on the body. No footprints or hoof prints to hint one of the native tribes had discovered the baby and made off with it.

A fierce gust of wind kicked up. Maybe the woman was delusional and there was no child. Baby or not, the temperature continued to grow colder. He glanced up at the darkening clouds. If the woman was to survive, he needed to get her to shelter.

He secured the buckles of the large chest and hefted it onto his shoulder. Walking as fast as the heavy weight allowed, he hurried to where he'd left the girl. There he set the trunk next to the tree. He'd send his handyman to retrieve it and to continue searching for the missing child.

Kneeling, he touched her shoulder. "Ma'am, I'm taking you to my home. But first, I need to get you on my horse. Can you steady yourself in the saddle until I can mount behind you?"

Her eyes fluttered, and she nodded.

He hadn't noticed before, when he'd carried her from the creek, but now, with her in his arms, the scent of roses reached him. When he inhaled the light fragrance, he decided the dropping temperature had muddled his mind.

A rose in early spring made no sense to him, yet she smelled of flowers, and even with the ashen tinge to her cheeks and her colorless lips, she reminded him of a porcelain doll that his little sister had cherished. The memory of a freckle-faced little girl with a winning smile riffled over him and just as quickly faded.

The young woman weighed no more than a feather as he lifted her to the saddle. He placed her hands around the horn and instructed her to hold tight while he toed his boot into the stirrup and swung up behind her.

Wrapping her against his chest, he gigged the gelding into a lope. She sighed. "How far?"

He didn't think telling her was wise. "Rest and think pleasant thoughts. We'll be there in the wink of an eye."

****

She dreamed of the face leering at her. His eyes were as cold and menacing as the poisonous viper that had stared at her. His smile was pure evil, as were his hands touching, probing, hurting, even as she protested. He was the devil who had beguiled her with his fancy words and sweet promises. Lies...all lies.

The expression he wore sent a chill of dread down her spine. She shook her head, denying what was happening, his hand over her mouth to muffle her cries. His voice sounded as if he spoke from far away—the words distorted accusations. *Don't go all innocent on me, Libby.* He'd laughed. *You begged for it...every time I looked at you.*

A pair of hands reached for her. Fear coiled in her stomach.

She screamed.

****

The woman jerked upward. Her head hit Ethan on the chin. He blinked away the painful surprise and tightened his arm, forcing her against his chest.

She whispered, "Don't...not again."

He thought her voice sounded odd, deep, and rusty, and her body trembled with a raging fever. He hushed her with the promise that she was safe.

Luck was on Ethan's side. A full moon allowed him to ride the long distance at a full gallop. A mile from the homestead, a spark of light appeared in the distance. It moved like a bouncing ball. His breath seized in his throat. He forced his body to relax. The Osage and Shawnee were friendly. Nonetheless, he hauled against the reins, pulling the dun gelding to a halt in a stand of trees.

She shivered against his chest. "Where are we?"

He shushed the girl. "Close your eyes and rest."

A voice called out. "Ethan...Ethan Wheeler."

He urged the horse forward. "Luther, by damn, I'm glad to see you."

The old man held the torch high. "Who in tarnation have you got there?"

Ethan blew out a tired sigh. "Don't know. She's been moccasin-bit, down by Osage Creek. Surely am relieved to meet up with you."

The older man held the torch high. "I feared when Stubborn came running into the yard like the Comanche were after him that something bad had happened. I see it did."

"Is Jacob okay?"

"Don't fret. He's sound asleep. Checked on him before I left."

Ethan nodded. "Listen, Luther, this woman keeps rambling about a baby. I did a quick scout about and didn't find sign of one. Maybe she's delusional from the venom. Anyhow, ride on to the creek and use what light you have to search high and low. I'll do what I can to make her comfortable."

"Gall dang it, Ethan. A baby, you say? The poor critter'll freeze to death, or worse."

"Get a move on. I'll wake Jacob and send him to get Big John's wife."

"B-but, Ethan, she's a-a…"

"A woman, Luther. It don't matter that she's Shawnee. Redfern Finnegan is John's legal wedded wife. Besides, I can't be undressing a gentle lady down to her jaybird suit. It's unchristian."

"What if I don't find the baby…what then?"

Ethan drew in a deep breath and squared his shoulders. "There's a large steamer trunk under a tree by the creek. Bring it to the house. We'll figure how to break the unfortunate news when the time is right. All the more reason to have another woman present."

"Yep, I reckon you're right 'bout that."

As the handyman put the spurs to his horse, he yelled over his shoulder, "Jest so you know, I hung the deer in the ice house. The meat didn't go rancid. It'll keep until we can skin it out proper."

Luther's words ignited an idea in Ethan's mind. He'd once heard a mountain man tell how he'd survived a bear attack by packing himself in snow to slow the bleeding. Maybe the temperature in the ice house would have the same effect on poison.

Chapter Two

Ethan sprinted into the cabin and climbed the ladder to the loft. "Jacob, wake up, son. Dress in your warmest clothes and meet me at the barn. Jacob...do you hear me?"

Sleepy-eyed and yawning, the eight-year-old sat up and scratched through a mop of russet hair. "Is it dawn already, Pa? Seems like I just went to sleep."

"I found a woman down by the creek. She's snake bit and needs doctoring. I put her in the ice house."

The boy scrambled from his goose-down pallet. "Gosh, Pa. A woman...in the ice house? She'll freeze her taters off."

Ethan backed down the wooden ladder, then stepped up one rung. "Don't forget your toboggan and gloves. Wouldn't want *your* taters to freeze." He winked a smile at the freckled face. "Meet me in the barn."

Closing the cabin door, Ethan shoved his hands into his pockets and bent his head against the wind as he sprinted through a light blanket of snow toward the barn. Inside, the horses nickered a welcome, and the milk cow lowed. Intense concern tightened his heart at the thought of sending his son on a twenty-mile night ride, and on Bucephalus. Jacob had named the black stallion after hearing the story about the boy king Alexander and his mighty steed.

When Ethan opened the stall door, the thoroughbred stallion blew and pawed the floor. Ethan clasped both sides of the halter straps and looked the horse in the eye. "Just like Bucephalus took care of Alexander, I trust you to do the same for my son. He's all I have left in this world."

The horse squealed and tried to back away. The three-year-old stallion was barely broke to saddle. Ethan cursed under his breath. Damn the woman for interrupting his life, for placing him in a position to risk his son's safety.

By some mercy, some cruelty of fate on this chilly spring night, Ethan tamped down the dread building like a brush fire as he wondered why he'd happened across a woman who looked like an angel. Was she a diseased harlot who'd been run out of town? No, the town of Mineola had no such establishments that employed that type of woman. He brushed that thought away. Sometimes wagon trains passed several miles outside of town; maybe the woman had committed a crime and was banished? Nope, he concluded that anyone who was as frail and beautiful and angelic-looking as she was couldn't have done anything to warrant banishment.

Puzzling over the mystery, he grabbed the saddle and blanket from the rack and eased it onto the sleek back. The stallion rolled its eyes and stepped sideways as if to avoid the large foreign object held in the man's hands.

Behind Ethan, Jacob's skeptical voice said, "Pa…am I ridin'…Cephus?"

Ethan spoke calming words to the big horse as he fastened the cinch strap. He glanced over his shoulder and smiled at the owlish dismay in his son's brown eyes, eyes that matched his mother's, God rest her soul. She lay under the sweet gum tree, along with a daughter and an infant son.

"Your pony is too old for a long hard ride. Both of the mares are due to foal any day, and my horse hasn't had time to rest. You're not afraid, are you?"

The youngster puffed out his chest. Ethan swallowed the chuckle in his throat at the indignant frown scowling at him. "I'm eight. 'Course I ain't scared." Then the boy looked down and kicked a dirt clod. "Well, maybe a little. Does that make me a coward, Pa?"

Ethan gathered the youngster and hugged him hard. "The bravest men are the ones who own up to being afraid." He lifted the boy into the saddle, and while adjusting the stirrups to fit a pair of short legs, he talked. "I'll lead you to the edge of the yard. Before I turn loose, hunker down in the saddle so Cephus doesn't jump out from under you. Don't hold him back. If you have to, lean forward and wrap your hands in his mane to keep from falling off, but let 'im run."

He pulled a folded note from his pocket and tucked it inside his son's jacket. "Give this to Redfern or Big John." He laid a hand on Jacob's leg. "Give Cephus a good rubdown before you stable him, but no feed and no water until he's cooled off. We don't want to founder him. And you, my brave boy, will spend the night there. Don't ride home. I'll send Luther for you in the morning."

The lad swallowed hard and nodded. Ethan blew out a heavy sigh. His heart pounded against his ribs. He wanted his son tucked safely in bed, dreaming little-boy dreams—not hanging on for dear life astride a horse that could outrun a locomotive pulling ten rail cars, and without breaking into a lather.

****

She awakened only once during the night. The back of her was warm enough, but her chest and arms and legs were freezing. If this were hell, then she wondered why her teeth chattered from the cold.

The instinctual urge to open her eyes had long since faded. Turning inward, she called forth the face of the man who had sentenced her to purgatory. She would choose death before allowing him to touch her again.

He had stolen her future, her freedom, and destroyed her dignity. Even though she had thwarted his advances, he had continued his testament of how much he loved her.

The pain in her arm increased. She swallowed the nausea that scalded the sides of her throat. Mercy, she was scared. In truth, she wasn't overly afraid of death. It was the melancholic process of dying that came before that terrified her. It was the thought of her own behavior before the shameful deed was completed that made her want to crawl into a hole, never to greet the light of day again. She had finally believed that he truly loved her. He had convinced her that his wife was as frigid as a winter's day, devoid of love, and had threatened to divorce him once they arrived in California. He had read poetry, beautiful romantic sonnets that had spoken to her innocence. Her fault...all her fault. She was an intelligent woman. *I should have known. Oh, God, I should have known he only wanted to use me.*

She was tired, more tired than she'd ever been in

her life.

An ominous creak of an opening door sent new chills skittering across her flesh. She opened her eyes to the dark. A lantern swung into view, blinding her even with its muted glow. She grasped a glimmer of hope, because it was all she had. The figure that towered over her wasn't *him*.

A woman's face came into view. "She's awake." And then, offering a reassuring smile, a melodic voice said, "I am Redfern Finnegan, and this is my friend, Ethan Wheeler. Can you tell us your name?"

She shifted her gaze toward Ethan. She wasn't certain she could utter a sound. "I remember you from the creek. My name is Liberty Trivette." The blankets had absorbed much of the room's dampness, but she felt as if she were draped across a block of ice. Her teeth chattered. "I'm v-very c-cold."

She didn't have time to gasp. With lightning speed, Ethan lifted her into his arms. She felt his warmth against her cheek, almost hot, and terribly inviting to snuggle against. He smelled good, too, like leather and male, and she couldn't help but react. She was suffering delusions from the snake bite. For certain, that was the reason his closeness was having such an unsettling effect on her. Why else was her heart racing?

His breath heated the side of her neck, comforting her. How could this be? She was confused; nothing was making sense to her anymore. Liberty shook her head, determined to shake the sleepy feeling invading her. "P-put me down. I'm going to be sick."

The debilitating ache in her abdomen increased. She groaned as she reached toward Redfern and sobbed. "My baby. Please don't let my baby die."

The despair in Ethan's voice was evident. "I swear, ma'am, I looked high and low for your child. My handyman is still searching."

Liberty placed a hand on her abdomen. "No, you don't understand..."

Sickness rippled up Liberty's throat, and before she could swallow it down, a frothy yellow substance spewed against Ethan's jacket. From a faraway place, she heard the Indian woman's voice. "Hurry, Ethan. We need to get her to the house."

Pain engulfed her. Liberty cried out as the relentless agony ripped through the nether regions of her womanhood. "Oh, God...please...no more. Just let me die."

Her body jostled painfully against Ethan's chest as he raced to the cabin. He apologized for hurting her. Once inside, Redfern rushed to the bed and stripped off the quilt. "Do you have an old blanket?"

He indicated the chest against the wall. Her movements rapid and sure, Redfern readied the bed. "I'll need hot water and fresh linen torn into strips to stanch the bleeding." Redfern opened her medicine bag. "I'll brew a tea of motherwort. It will help bring forth the birth."

"Ethan!" Redfern chastised him for what appeared as wool-gathering. "Don't stand there. I need hot water and bandages."

Understanding slammed against his gut. He'd witnessed his wife going through this same painful ordeal more times than he wanted to remember. "You mean she's miscarrying?"

"Life is cruel sometimes." Redfern gave him an empathic smile.

His broad shoulders tensed beneath the gray wool shirt. "How will we tell her?"

"As gently as possible. Quickly, get me a cup of warm water." Redfern smoothed Liberty's sweaty brow.

Before he could rush to do the Shawnee woman's bidding, Liberty's body arched high off the mattress. She screamed, "I condemn him to hell for what he did to me!"

Redfern spoke soothingly. "Your husband?"

"I have no husband." Liberty panted as she clutched the sides of the bed frame.

In her painful delirium and between gasps, Liberty revealed how Byron Stanwyck had forcibly violated her, not once, but several times.

Ethan returned with the cup of hot water. He watched the Shawnee woman crush leaves of motherwort between her palms and use the spoon to swirl the liquid until it became a potent brew.

A sound of disgust erupted from Ethan's throat. "Man like that ought to be hung up and gelded." He supported Liberty's body while Redfern encouraged her to down the entire cup of bittersweet liquid.

Between sobs and hiccups, Liberty related how her father had died unexpectedly and how Stanwyck had used her aloneness to his advantage, making her think he was her friend. "His wife was with child. She was a frail, pallid woman and sick every morning." Liberty loosed a strangled sob. "He often professed his love for me and said a man needed loving back. He said once we arrived in California, he would divorce her." The cords in Liberty's neck turned blue from the strain. "He even promised to marry me. I didn't want his promises.

I didn't want his advances. When I told him I was with child and threatened to tell his wife what he'd done to me, Byron called a meeting, and in front of all the people on the wagon train, he called me a jezebel. He said I had seduced him, and with his wife being in the family way and sick, he'd been weak of the flesh and had fallen prey to my promiscuous wiles."

Tears laced her eyelashes. "Before him...I had never..." She bit her lower lip, and the tears flowed. "He took what didn't belong to him. What man will want me now?"

Liberty closed her eyes. Her breathing steadied.

"The potion is easing her pain." Redfern used a damp cloth to cool Liberty's sweaty brow.

Sorrow and anger filled Ethan. He held Liberty's hand but spoke to no one in particular. "I watched my wife die from grief over too many babies that died before they were born. It pains me to have to plant another cross on the hilltop."

Liberty opened her eyes and looked into his blue ones, which held kindness, and empathy, and his own personal pain. She watched his jawline flex, and flex again. Even in the anguish and agony of losing her baby, she felt a jolt at Ethan's touch.

Liberty's body tensed again. The pain of the miscarriage peaked. She thrashed from side to side, not trying to suppress her moans or half-screams, and then there was relief as the lifeless being slipped from her body. Soon afterward, darkness closed over her. Peaceful, pain-free darkness. She shut her eyes, too weary to keep them open.

Chapter Three

Two days later, Ethan stood in the yard watching the wagon bump along the road that led to his house. His son sat beside a bear of a man. The sleek black stallion trotted behind the wagon.

Ethan raised his hand in a friendly greeting as he called over his shoulder, "Big John's come to take you home, Redfern."

She stepped from the porch. "More likely he's come for a good meal. John is handy at many things, but not at cooking."

"Whoa, hoss." John pulled the wagon to a halt. "Woman, me and this yar boy are hungry enough to eat a stack of flapjacks a mile high." He turned to Jacob and grinned. "Ain't that right, boy?"

Jacob returned the grin. He rubbed his stomach. "Anything but beans."

Laughter filled the yard, and Ethan reached up for his son. "Any problems with Cephus?"

Jacob's grin grew wider. "He wasn't even breathin' hard when I got to Mr. Finnegan's place."

"This yar young'n had his hands wrapped so tight in that stallion's mane, thought I'd have to cut 'im free. Right proud ye ought to be of the boy, Ethan. After he delivered your message, he wouldn't come into the house until he'd cooled out the hoss. Hellfire, that long-legged sonofagun hadn't broke a sweat, even after runnin' twenty miles."

Pride swelling his chest, Ethan hugged his son. "C'mon, let's help John unhitch his team while Redfern puts the finishing touches on breakfast."

"How's that lady, Pa? Did ya find her baby?"

Ethan ruffled the mop of red hair. "She's much better, and the baby wasn't lost. She…well…her baby is like the ones up on the hill."

The smile clouded from the youngster's eyes. Ethan knew his son understood about the little graves under the sweet gum tree. "I reckon she's sad, ain't she, Pa?"

Redfern stepped to the porch. A cold wind had kicked up. "You men get on with your business and then come inside before you catch your death. And round up Luther. He'll be needin' coffee to heat up his innards." She steered Jacob toward the front door. "Whilst I fix you a cup of warm milk laced with honey and cinnamon, you can take this food to Miss Trivette."

She placed the tray in the boy's outstretched hands and guided him toward the closed bedroom door. "If she's sleeping, just leave the tray on the table by the bed." Redfern quietly opened the door.

Jacob whispered, "Gosh, she's pretty."

Liberty sat propped against the headboard, and her face brightened into a smile when she saw the boy.

"I brung you some food." He carefully allowed the pale-faced woman to relieve him of his burden.

"That's kind of you. What's your name?"

"Jacob." He scrunched his face into a frown as he looked at the bowl of clear broth and the cup of steaming tea. "Wouldn't you rather have flapjacks? Redfern makes 'em real fluffy."

Liberty sighed. "Truthfully, I'm not very hungry. You can eat my share of pancakes."

"Okay." Jacob walked back toward the door and placed his hand on the knob. He hesitated and turned. "My mama is in heaven. I think she'll take care of your baby." With that he left Liberty to her thoughts.

Liberty's throat constricted. She let her head fall back against the pillow. Her eyes tightly shut, she struggled with mixed emotions. One part of her mind was filled with deep sorrow for the child she would never hold in her arms; the other part of her wondered if she could have loved a baby sired by a depraved monster.

Even now she could hear Byron's mocking laughter. She placed both hands over her face to shut out the image of his sneering grin.

The chicken broth's aroma served as a reminder that it had been a long while since her last meal. In fact, she didn't remember how long it had been since she'd eaten. Her stomach was ravenously hungry, her emotions almost too raw to eat. Her stomach won the battle.

She lay there trembling and weeping softly. She thought about Redfern Finnegan's parting words: "You'll find no better man than Ethan Wheeler. I did not know my Big John when he traded ten horses to my father as a bride-price for me. I have borne him three strapping sons, and I have come to love John more than the moon and the stars." The Shawnee woman had patted Liberty's hand. "Unless you have money and family, there isn't much of a future on the prairie for a woman without a good man."

Sadness had settled over Liberty. As she had

looked imploringly into Redfern's plain but radiant face, all her thoughts and fears must have been apparent, for the Indian woman had said, "You need not make any sudden decisions today. And remember, you are not a prisoner. If you ask, Ethan will drive you to Mineola. From there you can catch a stagecoach to wherever it is you wish to go."

And then Redfern had asked, "Where were you bound?"

"My father was a professor of English literature. He was also a dreamer. He sold everything we owned to follow his dream of starting a small university in California. He spent most of the money to purchase the wagon and supplies for the trip, and then there was the fee to Mr. Hardesty, the wagon master. In truth, we were almost penniless. Father was fond of saying we were traveling on a hope and a prayer."

Redfern nodded. "Your father spoke wise words." She patted Liberty's hand. "Time will heal the despair in your heart, and then you will be ready to seek a husband."

Liberty stared at the Shawnee woman a long time. Then, calmly and slowly, she said, "I don't want a husband. In fact, I don't want any man. Not now. Not ever."

"Of course. Rest now." On silent feet, Redfern had left the room.

Liberty cried harder. She didn't know what to do or where to go. Her mother had succumbed to a fever shortly after Liberty's birth; her father had died unexpectedly on the trail. Byron Stanwyck had stolen what little money she had. All her earthly belongings lay in the large wooden chest. She had no family to turn to. She did not sleep that night, but tossed and turned, wondering what was to become of her now.

****

Hours after the Finnegans had returned to their ranch, and night had fallen, Ethan shared the loft with his sleeping son. Hands tucked behind his head, his mind rested on the woman who slept in his bed. A deep loneliness filled him. How long had it been since he'd buried his wife? He calculated the age of his son with the years of her passing. Three years. Three years to grieve. Three years of aloneness. Three years without the comfort of a woman. Life was ugly and unfair.

He closed his eyes, remembering. His manhood had lain fallow all these years, and now it reared alive and bucked against his belly. He needed comforting; he ached for it.

He had looked in on Liberty before retiring to the loft. She had been awake. His eyes had met hers with a brief but potent intensity. She had lifted a hand to brush aside a stray wisp of golden hair. He'd wanted to run his fingers through it, to frame her face with his hands. Even now he could smell the scent of rose petals. Her scent.

Another thing he didn't want to think about was her mouth. He could only imagine how it would be to kiss her lips. His heart twisted.

Ethan controlled the wild sudden desire to climb down the ladder and go to her. This was more than lust. He felt a deep and urgent need to protect her, to make her his. And then it came to him, lying there in the dark, listening to the soft pattering of his son's snores, that Liberty Trivette had wended her way into his heart. Was it love? How could it be, when he didn't know her and she didn't know him?

He knew she'd leave even though she had no place to go. With a ragged sigh, he shifted to a more comfortable position, drifting to sleep while formulating a plan to win her heart.

Chapter Four

Liberty enjoyed each day of her recuperation. She looked forward to Jacob's daily visits and then the evening chats with Ethan and the challenge of trying to defeat him at games of chess. A fortnight had passed since surviving the snake bite and the misery of her miscarriage. If felt good to stretch her legs after days of being cooped up inside the house. She lifted her face to the morning sun and smiled.

"It's a lovely day." Liberty sighed. "I don't wish to continue imposing on your hospitality."

"Truthfully, it's nice having a woman around, especially for Jacob."

Ethan reached down and plucked a handful of wild daisies. He was broad-shouldered, slim-hipped, and male, and there was a sad tiredness in his eyes. She put aside an impulsive desire to lean closer to him.

"How long has it been since your wife passed away?" She accepted the flowers and lifted them to her nose.

Ethan grew quiet.

Liberty followed his gaze toward the hilltop marked with crosses. "I'm sorry to dredge up sorrowful memories. Losing a loved one is heartbreaking."

He let out a long breath. "If you don't mind my asking, had your father been sick long before his passing?"

She turned her head away for a moment, struggling to compose herself. "I'm not sure. Father was never a complainer. He'd always brush away my concerns when I questioned him." She expelled a long sigh. "He tried to hide the pain in his chest, and then one evening we were sitting around the campfire, listening to our fellow travelers' music." She went silent for a moment. "It was so odd. Father stood, offered me his hand, and called me—Lizette. That was my mother's name. In the blink of an eye, he wilted to the ground, and he was gone."

She struggled against the tears. "Although it's been little more than a fortnight, in some ways it seems like an eternity." She gathered the flowers against her chest. "I truly miss him."

Ethan cleared his throat. "How long had you been alone before I happened upon you?"

Liberty gathered her thoughts. "Two days, I think. I still can't believe no one protested my being left behind—cast out on the word of a...a fiend. But Byron was as beguiling as the devil. Even the older, more mature women fell over themselves just to get a smile from him. In my heart, I believe his wife knew what he'd done to me."

Ethan took Liberty's hand in his. "Why do you suppose she didn't speak up on your behalf?"

Liberty snatched her hand away as if his touch had scorched her, while she tried to keep the bitterness from her voice. "Jane Ann was pregnant. She was also sickly and bedridden most of the trip. Besides, not only is Byron a successful attorney, he is the son of one of the richest men in Maryland. Jane Ann Stanwyck knew all too well which side her bread was buttered on. Of course she wasn't about to speak out against her husband to defend me."

Ethan shuffled his feet, then mumbled something about her continuing on.

"No one can imagine the anger and the fear I felt as the wagons rolled off, leaving me standing there— alone. I watched until they were out of sight, hoping beyond hope that someone would turn around and return for me.

"When they didn't, I started walking without any idea where I was going. The longer I dragged the trunk, the heavier it seemed to get, until I couldn't drag it anymore. I was so thirsty. That's when I saw the creek, and...you know the rest." She stood a little straighter, though her chin wobbled. "I've never really thanked you for all you've done for me. Mere words hardly seem enough."

He cocked an eyebrow, his fair hair gilded by the sunlight, and Liberty thought she'd never seen a more handsome man in her entire life. Her heart skipped a couple of beats and the pulse at the base of her throat beat so hard she coughed.

"No thanks is needed, Miss Trivette. It pleasures me to see you help my son with his reading and numbers. That's payment enough."

A long silence passed before Ethan spoke. "Now that you're well enough to travel, I suppose you'll want to get to California."

Liberty bit her lower lip, hesitating. In truth, she was flat broke. Byron Stanwyck had stolen what little funds she possessed.

Ethan cleared his throat. "Miss Trivette, if it's money you need for stage fare, well, I've a bit put aside."

She didn't know what to say. "I'd much prefer it if you would call me Liberty."

"Yes, ma'am, Liberty." His eyes met hers with brief but potent intensity. "It's not really my business, but the man who hurt you—"

She held up her hand to stop Ethan. She remembered the cold fury of Byron's violence. Her voice rasped. "You're right. It's not your business. I'd prefer to put him and the entire sordid incident out of my mind." She turned to walk back toward the house.

Ethan reached out and cupped her elbow. "My apologies; the offer still stands if you need stage fare. As soon as you feel well enough to travel, I'll drive you into town. No hurry, of course."

His palm was warm and snug against her arm. When he looked at her, it wasn't easy to speak. So different from Byron; so different from her father.

"You have already been more than generous, Mr. Wheeler...Ethan. I do wish to fulfill my father's dream of founding a university. And, of course, once I acquire suitable employment, I will find a way to repay you."

The silence between them seemed ominous. She depended on this man's hospitality and needed to refrain from offending him further. She opened her mouth to ask if staying another few days would be an inconvenience, but an exuberant voice interrupted her.

"Pa...Pa!" Grinning from ear to ear, Jacob held up a string of brook trout. "Look at what me and Luther caught. There's enough for supper."

Ethan left her and sprinted forward to kneel before his son. "That's a right nice catch you have." Love and pride mingled in his voice.

Liberty found herself skipping forward. She stared down at the little boy. "It's about time I earn my keep for another few more days at least." She squelched the squeamish shiver. "Maybe you'd teach me how to clean fish?"

Liberty almost laughed out loud at Jacob's dubious glance. "Gosh, you ain't gonna throw up or faint, are ya?"

"*You're not* going to throw up or faint, are you?" she corrected.

Jacob scrunched his face into a frown. "Ain't that what I just said?"

This time, Liberty did laugh. "Come on, we'll work on proper grammar later. We have fish to clean."

Ethan caught her hand. He mouthed, *Thank you.*

****

Ethan stood in the shadows of the barn door, watching his son patiently teach Liberty how to clean fish. He admired the woman whose expression plainly indicated that scooping out fish guts and having fish scales splatter over the front of her pretty yellow dress was not her idea of afternoon fun.

That was the moment he truly fell in love with her, though he didn't know it.

Liberty must have sensed he was watching her. She glanced toward the barn and, with a slight shrug of her shoulders, shot him a weak smile, then grabbed another fish. In the sunlight her hair was the color of rich golden honey. He yearned to run his fingers through it, and to frame her face with his hands. Desire tore at him, and he suppressed it.

"Ain't that somethin'." Luther's voice startled Ethan. "Iffen I were you, I'd be thinkin' 'bout sparkin' that young woman. Jacob needs a ma, and a man cain't live on fish alone." The old man let out a quiet guffaw.

Ethan tucked his hands inside his pants pockets. His eyes brooked no nonsense as he faced the older man. "Don't go putting ideas in the boy's head. Miss Trivette as much as said she'll be leaving soon. I won't have my son hurt. You hear me, Luther?"

The handyman lifted the battered hat and scratched his head. "I love that boy like he was my own. I'd cut my right arm off before bringin' harm to him. Didn't mean to run off at the mouth." He turned on his heel and disappeared inside the barn.

Ethan swallowed. He was still chewing on what Luther had said about a man not being able to live on fish alone. In all the hard times, and even when he'd buried his wife, he had never sought solace in a bottle. But now he needed a drink. Something stronger than coffee.

Chapter Five

Liberty awoke feeling out of sorts. She brushed off the dizziness and slight headache as a mixture of excitement and anxiety. Today Ethan would drive her to town to catch the afternoon stage. She gathered her purse, and before leaving the bedroom gave it another quick look to make certain she hadn't forgotten anything and that she was leaving it in neat order.

Outside, Ethan was grimly silent as Liberty bent down to hug his son. "Practice your reading and numbers." Her voice cracked. "As soon as I'm settled, I'll send you my address. I hope you'll write and tell me all the news."

Jacob pulled from her arms. "Yes, ma'am."

Luther stood with his hat against his chest. "Sure hate to see ya go, Miss Liberty."

She kissed him on the cheek. "Thank you for all you've done, Luther."

After the tearful farewells, Ethan placed his hands around Liberty's waist to assist her onto the wagon. He sagged inwardly.

She turned in his arms. Her green eyes met narrowed blue eyes.

Ethan's jawline tightened. "It's not safe for a woman to travel alone."

Liberty drew a deep breath and released it. "I won't be alone. The coaches are generally full, aren't they?"

Ethan folded his arms against his chest. "Yes, full of fast-talking whiskey drummers and gamblers, and you never know when outlaws might attack the stage."

Liberty looked up at the sun as if trying to gauge the time. "Help me up, Ethan. I'm going to California, and that's that."

Liberty had donned a matronly brown traveling suit. A pert hat with a veil to hide her face adorned her crown of blonde hair. In spite of the warm day and the cape draped over her shoulders, she shivered and risked a sidelong glance at Ethan, who was close enough to see her face through the veiling. He was scowling.

****

She remembered the depth of blue in Ethan's eyes, and the frown on his face. She remembered the odd buzzing in her ears, and the sun spots that seemed to pierce through the veiling. She didn't remember fainting.

Days passed into weeks. Liberty suffered several bouts of fever that left her weak and bedridden, with Ethan tending her.

The first morning of May was fresh with the scent of wildflowers and the humming of bees. The sun continued to rise. Ethan turned the stallion out to pasture and leaned against the corral, watching the big black horse prance around the pasture.

"Yer like a sore-tailed bear who woke up grumpy from a winter's sleep."

Lost in thought, Ethan raised an eyebrow at the comment. "What the hell are you talking about, Luther?"

The old man chuckled. "I'm nigh on seventy years, but I ain't so old that I've forgotten what it's like to hold a good woman in my arms. I still miss my Edith. Miss her cookin', miss the way she smelled after bread-makin' and pie-bakin' days, miss cuddlin' and the lovin' that a man and woman share in private. My Edith was winter and sunshine all mixed together. I was already an old man when the good Lord called her home. Won't never be another like her, and at my age I ain't cravin' another."

Ethan frowned at the man. "What's your point, Luther?"

The old man loosed an exasperated sigh. He pointed to where Liberty and Jacob sat under a large shade tree, their heads bent toward a book. "It's writ all over her face every time she looks at you. And you, you reek with the odor of dee-sire. I'm tellin' you, Ethan, it ain't healthy for a man to five-finger himself to sleep at night."

Ethan balled a fist. "Mind your tongue, Luther."

The old man held his ground. He nodded toward the tree. "Then you best think 'bout Jacob. It's been nigh on to a month since you brought her back here. The boy's gettin' mighty attached to Miss Liberty." Luther scratched beneath his hat. "You're a smart man, Ethan. You figure it out." With that, he sauntered off to the barn.

Ethan shifted his gaze toward the sounds of laughter. Apparently forgotten, the pages of a book fluttered in the breeze while his son and Liberty chased a butterfly. The sight both warmed him and disturbed him. Damn Luther for his old-man wisdom.

He called, "Luther…"

The handyman simply waved and kept walking. "No time to talk. Chores don't do theirselves."

Laughter turned Ethan back to watch Liberty. She held her skirt high as she chased after his son. He thought about the day he'd found her, and the way he'd lifted her skirt to rip strips of cloth from her undergarment. The reminder of the soft, smooth skin that lay beneath those frilly underthings brought an ache, a sudden rush of blinding desire that weakened Ethan's knees.

In that brief moment of need came a deeper, gut-gripping emotion. He watched as Jacob handed Liberty a single yellow flower. She gathered the little boy in her arms and hugged him, and Jacob had not shied away. In that instant Ethan's heart overflowed with love. The realization brought his heart into his throat just to look at her.

Later in the afternoon, Redfern and Big John rode into the yard. John helped his wife down from the wagon. Liberty greeted the Shawnee woman with a slight kiss to each cheek. At the woman's startled look, Liberty quickly explained, "My father and mother were French. Kissing on each cheek is a customary greeting."

Big John patted his bearded face. "I think I like that custom."

Redfern playfully batted her husband on the arm. "We're on our way home from Mineola. The Abernathys are holding a barn-raising celebration next Saturday. Everyone's invited. There'll be music and dancing, and games for the young and old. All the visiting women are asked to bring a covered dish and a dessert."

"Pa, can we go?" Jacob's voice exuded excitement.

It seemed all eyes looked toward Ethan. He glanced at Liberty. She held fisted hands against her breasts. He swore apprehension hung heavy in her eyes. Was she afraid of what people might say—if they would judge her, an unwed woman living with a man and his son? News was a commodity in remote areas, and a year-old newspaper worn thin from being passed around by many hands was a welcomed rarity. Word had surely spread about Liberty, making her fodder for adulterated gossip. Luther's earlier words of wisdom drifted over Ethan. A social event presented the perfect opportunity to begin courting Liberty.

Ethan rubbed his hands together. "Liberty baked a skillet apple pie. It should be cool enough to cut."

"With cinnamon icing, and I got to lick the bowl," Jacob offered with a wide grin.

Liberty blushed. "Of course, and there is fresh coffee."

"But, Pa," the eight-year-old reminded, "you ain't said if we're going to the barn raising or not."

"*Haven't* said," Liberty corrected Jacob with a wink and a smile. She invited Redfern into the house to help with the pie.

Ethan's grin widened. "Of course we're going. It'll do us good to have a bit of fun."

Inside the cabin, Liberty counted out the saucers and forks. "Redfern, do you think people hereabouts know I'm a…a houseguest and nothing more?"

The Shawnee woman sliced the pie while Liberty filled the cups with rich amber coffee. "Probably."

A blush heightened the pink in Liberty's cheeks. "Will they treat me like a fallen woman?"

Redfern seemed to weigh the question before answering. "A timid rabbit is prey for the wolf. If the rabbit stays in its burrow, the wolf will find a way to ferret it out. But if the rabbit doesn't want to be eaten, it must be smarter than the wolf."

Liberty scrunched her face in confusion at the parable. "I think I understand. I should not be like the timid rabbit." Her courage wavered. "Are you and John attending?"

Redfern filled the last cup. "Don't fret yourself. I will help keep the wagging tongues at bay."

"I mean no offense, Redfern, but did other women treat you…" Liberty shrugged without finishing the thought, but an apology. "I'm sorry. That was rude of me."

"You mean because I'm Shawnee?" Redfern seemed to drift away for a moment. "At first it was difficult. It took a while to prove that I wasn't a renegade out to slit anyone's throat."

"How did you get people to accept you?"

"Any man who dared threaten me met the business end of John's fist." Redfern laughed with gusto. "In the long run, it was my knowledge of herbs, and cures for fevers, and child birthing that caused our neighbors to see me as a human and not a savage."

"Do you think Ethan would do the same for me?"

"Ethan is a man of honor."

The conversation was interrupted when the men entered the cabin, declaring they were hungry for pie.

When talk around the table ebbed from crops to foals and discussing who would attend the barn-raising festivities quieted, Ethan looked at Liberty. "I imagine being the daughter of a professor you attended a lot of fancy parties back East."

Liberty stood to collect the dishes and carry them to the sink. "Father was a fanciful man filled with notions and dreams. In truth, if it were not for the money I earned from tutoring, well..." She sighed and left the rest unsaid. "I've never been to a barn raising. What does one wear to such an event?"

Big John pushed back his chair. He pulled a pipe from his shirt pocket. "Let's leave the talk about fripperies and stuff to the ladies."

An hour later, Liberty stood in the yard with the men of her family, waving goodbye to their friends and attesting to seeing them on Saturday. When the lanterns were dimmed and the house was dark, she lay in Ethan's bed, staring up at the ceiling, toward where he shared the loft with his son. She lifted the blanket and inhaled the earthy scent of his masculinity. *The men of her family?* When had she begun to think of Ethan, Jacob, and even Luther as her family?

She felt an incomprehensible urge to have Ethan hold her, and she resisted it with all her might.

Chapter Six

In actuality, the neighboring men had met at the Abernathy farm on Friday to help build the barn walls and the roof. Saturday was saved for the festivities so the men would be rested and able to enjoy the party.

Liberty handed Jacob a basket filled with fresh-baked bread, wild strawberry jam, and two large meat-and-potato pies. A shiver of delight raced through her as Ethan placed his hands around her waist and lifted her down from the wagon. "I'm a bit nervous. What if the women don't accept me?"

Ethan offered what he hoped was a reassuring smile. "Most of the ladies are real nice. Most of them have a past, too. If anything, they'll be jealous of your beauty."

"Don't forget 'bout Miz Prudence, Pa. She always looks like she's been suckin' on sour lemons."

Liberty smothered the laughter at the image Jacob conjured of the woman. "*About*, Jacob, and *sucking*."

"Ain't that...um...isn't that what I just said? Ah, shucks, Miss Liberty."

She bent down and kissed his cheek. "Never mind." She made a shooing gestured. "Run on and have fun, but save at least one dance for me."

Jacob scampered off toward a group of boys about his age. He called their names, and they motioned him forward.

Redfern waved, dragging Big John with her. She linked arms with Liberty and issued a warning to the men. "We all know there are jugs. Mind how much you drink."

Big John placed a playful smack on his wife's backside. "Mind you don't let them boys of our'n eat up all the fried chicken in that thar basket yer holdin'."

Dusk quickly turned into dark. Lanterns were lit. Food was laid out on long planks, with punch for drinking with it. Happy voices filled the partially finished barn. Much to her discomfort, Liberty found herself the center of attention. Mrs. Gephart, who spoke with a distinct German accent, complimented Liberty's blue dress, while Mrs. Dunwoody wanted Liberty's recipe for the meat-and-potato pie. Liberty answered all questions—yes, she could play the piano, no, she didn't sing, yes, she had earned her teaching certificate and had planned to assist her father at the university he wanted to build.

All went well until Prudence Quattlebaum piped up with, "We heard you were snake bit. How is it you were down by the creek and got left by the wagon train?"

Liberty's throat constricted. Her heart skipped a beat. How did this woman know? She looked away for a moment, unable to bear the accusation in the woman's eyes.

Ethan gently cupped Liberty's elbow. He cast a warning glare at the reedy spinster who wore a perpetual sour expression. "I believe, Miz Prudence, that you have more than a few skeletons in your closet." He offered a sly grin. "Especially the one about a certain whiskey drummer and—"

The woman harrumphed and puffed up like a hen

ruffling her feathers. "Mind your business, Ethan Wheeler."

"Exactly, Miz Prudence. Now if you will excuse me." Ethan bowed his dismissal of the dour woman and then with a wink offered Liberty his hand. "The first dance is always a waltz. If your dance card isn't full, may I have the pleasure?"

Liberty folded into his arms as the guitar pickers and fiddle players plucked out the strands of a soulful waltz. Ethan kissed the top of her head and, even though the gesture was purely innocent, she felt a hot shiver shoot straight down to her womanhood, followed by a feeling of guilt.

She pulled back and stared into his pensive blue eyes. "How do you know about dance cards?"

He twirled her around and back into his arms. "I wasn't always a Missouri farmer. Nope. In New York, my father was a judge. My mother owned a millinery shop and catered only to the rich and sophisticated." He twirled her again and then back to him. "And I, my lady, was a budding lawyer."

Liberty drew back with an arched brow. "Why did you give up a lucrative career in a thriving city to come way out here?"

His breath tickled her ear as he spoke. "We all have our dreams, Liberty. Mine was to breathe fresh air, live in wide-open spaces, and be my own man. Being a lawyer was my father's choice for me. After the war, my needs grew stronger. And here I am."

"Your parents…do they still live in New York?"

"Yes, though my father has yet to forgive me for becoming a ne'er-do-well. Sadly, my mother is no longer with us."

Tears welled behind Liberty's eyes. "I'm sorry. I was an only child. Did you have siblings?"

He twirled her again. "I did. A sister named Penelope. She had a porcelain doll, aptly named Penny. She—my sister, that is—was full of life, and rambunctious. In many ways, Jacob favors her."

Ethan swept Liberty into his arms and expertly guided her around the room. "Where is Penelope now?"

The question was innocent enough. The answer was painful. "There was a fire... She died."

"I didn't mean to bring up painful memories."

Ethan offered a sad smile. "She was twelve. I was in Tennessee with my regiment when I got word about Penelope, and my mother." He drew a long breath. "It happened a long time ago."

Liberty was thankful when the tempo of the music changed. She couldn't bear the cold pain and fury that deepened the blue of Ethan's eyes to black.

A lively Virginia reel came after the waltz, and then a Scottish reel. Liberty couldn't remember when she'd had so much fun. Her toes hurt from being stepped on by heavy boots during the reels, and she was thirsty and breathless. "Ethan, do you mind if I step outside for a breath of air?"

"I could use some cooling off myself. I'll get us something cool to drink and join you."

She walked out into the inky darkness broken only by the light from the barn. The crisp air refreshed her as she sought solace in the thousands of glittering stars. Still she ached with strange longings and embarrassment at lewd thoughts.

****

Ethan stood in the shadows, holding a cup of

chilled punch in each hand. He watched as Liberty gazed at the stars. His Adam's apple traveled the length of his throat. There was no two ways about it, he loved this woman.

Before he could call back the words, he blurted out, "Liberty Trivette, will you be my wife? Tonight. Reverend and Mrs. Milford are here, and I'm certain Big John will stand up as my best man and Redfern for you."

When she faced him, he wasn't sure if her expression was one of total awe or complete disgust. What he did know was that in the moonlight she looked like an angel.

A smile lit her face, but she quickly frowned it away. "Oh, Ethan, I'm not a fit woman." She cupped his face with her hands. "I don't know when I fell in love with you, and I adore Jacob as if he was my own, but I've been ill used by another man. In time, you might come to hate me because I wasn't pure when I came to your bed."

She hugged herself as if beset by chills. "I couldn't bear it if you began to hate me. No, Ethan. I won't marry you."

He set away the cups of punch and folded her into his arms, his chin resting on her head. "All that matters is that I love you, Liberty Trivette. If you want, I'll get down on my knees and give you a proper proposal."

She bit her lip and looked away. "Oh, please, you don't understand."

He pointed toward the barn. Soft strains of another waltz filtered into the night. "Every man and woman inside has their own personal secrets. Don't judge yourself so harshly, Liberty."

He dropped to one knee and took her hand into his.

"Please stand up, Ethan. You are a good man, an understanding man."

He obeyed and with a deep chuckle said, "There are surely times when I wish I wasn't. This I will promise—I will never hurt you. Not deliberately." He hesitated, not knowing if he could live up to the next promise. "And...while I expect you to share my bed, I won't touch you until you are ready."

"Oh, Ethan, I don't understand why some woman hasn't already snapped you up."

His grin wobbled. "There's a barn full of them. You'd better hurry with making up your mind."

Moonlight glistened the tears that hung on Liberty's lashes. "Yes!" She flung her arms around his neck. "Yes, I will marry you." He felt her smile, like a light warming the cool darkness.

He touched his lips to hers; he kissed her long and hard, and they were both breathless when he finally broke away. "Let's go inside. We have an announcement to make."

She gripped his hand and followed him inside and to the stage, and waited while he whispered something to the man who seemed in charge of the musical group. He motioned Ethan to join him. The players did a musical rendition that beckoned the audience's attention.

Ethan stepped forward. He cleared his throat, not once but twice. "Friends...neighbors..." He pointed down at Liberty. "I've asked Miss Liberty Trivette to be my wife." He searched the crowd. "What better place to hold a wedding than right here, right now. I'd like Big John Finnegan and my son Jacob to stand beside me as my best men, and my bride-to-be would like Redfern Finnegan to be her matron of honor. Reverend Milford, will you perform the ceremony tonight?"

A portly man with salt-and-pepper gray fringe decorating an otherwise bald pate stepped through the crowd. He held a slice of cake in his hand. He brushed crumbs from his vest. "Just so happens I keep an extra marriage certificate or two tucked inside my Bible."

Cheers and whistles and applause filled the barn. Reverend Milford joined the happy couple. He pointed to where they should stand. "I suppose you have a ring?" He directed the question toward Ethan.

In a moment of panic, Ethan patted his pockets. He hadn't thought of a ring. In fact, when leaving to come to the party, proposing marriage had been the least thing on his mind. "I...I..."

Luther pushed through the bevy of people. He reached beneath his gray linen shirt and withdrew a silver chain that hung around his neck. A gold ring dangled from it. "My Edith wore this ring for nigh on forty years. It was her mother's before her. Ethan, yer like a son to me. It'd make me proud iffen you'd accept this as my weddin' present to you and Miss Liberty."

Tears welled in Liberty's eyes. She kissed the old man on the cheek. "It's a most precious gift that I will cherish always and forever."

The wedding took place in the barn with its freshly scented pine wood. Hay bales served as seats for the guests, and the band played a squeaky version of the wedding march.

It wasn't fear that caused the almost uncontrollable trembling of Liberty's body. No, it was the fear that in afterthought he might reject her that frightened her the most. After the I-do's, and the placing of the ring on her finger, Reverend Milford pronounced them husband and wife and generously invited Ethan to kiss the bride.

Ethan kissed Liberty almost the same way he had outside not more than a half hour ago. She was certain she would collapse from a combination of excitement and suffocation before he let her go.

And when he did, the Reverend Milford opened his hands toward the audience of smiling faces. "Ladies and gentlemen, may I present to you Mr. and Mrs. Ethan Wheeler."

Redfern leaned close and whispered, "Jacob and Luther will stay with us for a few days while you and Ethan get to know each other proper like."

Liberty was certain her cheeks would blister from the fierce way they heated. Unable to speak, she simply nodded her acquiescence.

****

Humming the bridal march and feeling happier than she'd ever expected, Liberty undid the buttons to the front of her blue dress. She hung it with care. Filling the basin with fresh water, she bathed with rose-scented soap. She uncoiled the braid and brushed her hair until it draped around her shoulders like waves of sun-kissed silk. Lastly, she slipped into her prettiest white cotton nightgown. She was thankful Ethan was giving her time alone to prepare for their wedding night. Earlier he had declared that he wouldn't touch her without her permission. She hoped he hadn't forgotten.

The night Byron Stanwyck had entered her wagon still haunted her. He hadn't waited until her father was cold in his grave before foisting his advances on her. There was no gentleness about him. He had pinched her and bitten her, and when he had entered her it was with such force that he'd placed his hand over her mouth to muffle her screams from the tearing, searing pain of her maidenhead. When he'd finished his rutting, he'd left her spent and sobbing and covered in blood.

She hugged herself to ward off the shivers that threatened to wrack her body. She plunged under the covers and pulled the quilt to her chin. Ethan appeared presently, carrying a lamp.

The mattress dipped as he sat on the edge and pulled off his boots. Liberty searched for something to say. Her nerves felt as if they were outside her body. "Thank you for staying in the barn while I bathed."

He undressed down to his underwear and climbed in beside Liberty as casually as if they had shared a bed for years. "Tomorrow I'll bring in the tub so you can have an all-over bath. When Luther returns, we'll go into Mineola and order lumber. We'll need to add another room to the house, and a bathing room, too. When our next child is born, it might be a little girl." He rolled to his side and twined a golden curl around his finger. "It's only fit and proper that the women in my house have a private place to bathe."

He loosed something like a strangled sigh. It seemed the pain in his eyes reflected her own. His voice dropped to a husky whisper. "I always intended to build a special room for Roberta, but somehow I never got around to it, and then it was too late."

There was something in the gentleness of his words that broke down the flimsy barriers she wanted to hide behind. Without warning she broke into sobs. She sensed Ethan was taken aback. But then he reached out and pulled her against his chest.

"Shh. Hush, now." He smoothed her hair. "Don't take on so, Libby. You'll hurt yourself."

She pushed from his arms. "Call me Liberty or call me nothing, but *never, ever* call me Libby! I despise that name."

Ethan drew his brows together. The venom in her voice took him by complete surprise.

She let out a small miserable wail. Her body was in a terrible turmoil. Part of her ached for Ethan to make love to her, and the other part refused to push Byron Stanwyck's leering face from her mind. She hiccupped between sobs. "It was *his* pet name for me."

She swallowed and angrily dashed away the tears with the back of her hand. "Hold me, Ethan. Just hold me."

He wrapped her in his arms. She laid her cheek against his chest. He felt strong, like a brick wall that could protect her from any storm. After a long while she said, "Make love to me, Ethan."

"Are you sure?"

She couldn't voice her answer and simply nodded. In the dark, he pressed her onto her back and leaned over her, his face no more than a shadow in the darkness of the bedroom.

He nuzzled her lips before fully taking them. He kissed her long and hard, and they were both breathless when he finally ended it. "I'll ask again—are you sure?"

"Y-yes," she managed to say. "I want you to love me the way a husband loves his wife."

Tears burned her eyes, and she was glad he couldn't see them. He held her a long time before his own need became too great. "Why are you crying,

Liberty?"

She didn't answer, couldn't answer.

"That man—the one before. It was your first time, and he hurt you, didn't he?"

She nodded, with a tired, woeful smile.

He hooked a finger under her chin so she was forced to look at him. "Not all men are animals. I'm sorry your first time left you hurt here." He touched her heart. "We don't have to do this until you are ready."

He rolled to his side, with his back to her. Liberty's heart slammed against her backbone. It wasn't fear of pain that held her back. No, it was the possibility of humiliation and rejection that frightened her so much. It was Ethan's gentle words that deepened the love she felt for him.

She exhaled a shaky breath. "I'm ready."

With great care, he straddled her thighs and rolled her nightgown up and over her head, tossing it to the floor. He looked into her face and down at her breast. "If you'll trust me, I promise to make it worthwhile."

Liberty felt shy and tried to cover her breasts. He gently pushed her hands aside. "Let me see you. All of you."

He touched one of her nipples, and it obediently hardened. He bent to suckle it.

She arched her back and moaned her pleasure. "I trust you."

He suckled her other breast, and at the same time he reached down to caress the moist delta between her thighs. When he trailed down her belly with moist kisses, she bit down on her fist to keep from crying out with pleasure.

He eased a finger deep inside her, and her body

bucked in a delicious spasm. Liberty spread her hands across his broad, muscled back and urged him closer. Ethan sighed and then very, very slowly glided himself into her.

She stilled. He whispered raspy words of comfort. "Shall I stop?"

She kissed the underside of his chin. "No," she whimpered. "Please—don't stop."

He gave her a moment to adjust herself to him before he began to move inside her, when her womb contracted in the throes of passion. A nearly suppressed chuckle bubbled from his throat, but she knew he wasn't making fun of her.

"Ethan," she murmured as her body lunged against his, "Ethan—is it supposed to be like this?" and she lunged again, meeting every parry of his hips.

This time he did laugh. "Yes, my sweet girl, it *is* supposed to be *just* like this." He plunged deep, and Liberty felt his seed spilling warm and strong through her.

The pleasure was so intense that by the time Ethan reached his pinnacle of satisfaction he collapsed beside her from the force of his release.

Liberty slipped her arms around her husband. She snuggled against him, her voice a mere whisper. "Thank you."

His eyes shone with desire. He cupped a breast, teasing the nipple between his fingers. "For what?"

"For taking me on the most delicious adventure I've ever experienced."

With a raw growl low in his throat, Ethan captured her lips. She gave a primitive guttural cry as he lunged inside her again, withdrew, and lunged again. She matched him thrust for thrust, and when her body began its dance of release, it seemed that her mind soared free of all the old fears.

Her body quivered with the aftershocks of release. Ethan was breathing hard, the tense muscles of his back moist under her palms. She kissed his forehead. "Will it always be like this?"

He rolled to his back, pulling her on top of him. He laughed and nipped at her nipple, sending waves of desire storming through her system again. "Until we are old and gray."

Liberty slid to his side. She closed her eyes, succumbing to exhaustion. However many years of love they had ahead of them, she intended to cherish every moment.

Chapter Seven

Liberty couldn't remember a time when she'd been so happy. Ethan reached over to tuck the lap blanket closer around her knees. She linked her arm through his and leaned her head against his broad shoulder. "I am extremely happy, and it's all because of you."

He cocked an eyebrow as he smiled at her. "I haven't done anything."

"Oh, but you have." She caressed the little mound beneath her coat. "You've given me love, a beautiful home *with* a bathing room, a soon-to-be school, and a baby. I'm the luckiest woman in the world."

Ethan kissed her on the forehead. "I saw the ocean once. Your eyes remind me of how green the water was, how warm and inviting. When you keep looking at me like that, I'm tempted to pull off the road to a nice secluded spot and make love to you."

She giggled like a schoolgirl. "Better take advantage of it while you can, mister. Pretty soon I'll be big as a cow and waddling around like a duck."

A frown crossed her face, and she grew somber. Ethan fretted. "What is it—the baby?"

She brushed away a sudden tear. "No...no, the baby is fine. It's just that—"

"Whoa." He hauled up on the reins and turned to face his wife. "Tell me, Liberty. No secrets, ever."

Liberty drew in a quivery breath. "It's all too

perfect. It makes me afraid."

"Afraid of what?"

She glanced around as if searching. "I don't know. It's like a premonition. What if he shows up?"

"He who, Liberty? I don't understand."

"Byron Stanwyck." A shiver raced down her spine. "It makes no sense, I know, but I have a feeling that one day he'll show up. The thought of seeing him frightens me."

Behind the light smile, she saw the concern in her husband's eyes. He clucked the horses into action. "Stanwyck is hundreds of miles from Missouri. It's October, and the wagon train should have arrived in California weeks ago."

"Of course." Logically, she knew Ethan was right. Still, she remembered Byron's dark expression and uncertain temper. She wanted to dissolve into tears; instead she smiled. "Redfern would say I'm having a case of baby nerves. Forgive me for being silly."

He gave her a reassuring pat on the knee.

Ethan had saved her, and because of him she had survived, she reminded herself. And she would keep on surviving. Innocence was gone, and it would take more than Byron Stanwyck to make her a simpering coward again.

"Can't you make these horses go any faster, husband? I think a bed would be much more comfortable than making love under a tree."

Ethan laughed deep in his throat. "Wife, you have lit a fire inside me that water won't put out." He clucked the horses to a trot.

She sighed, happy. There had been times in Philadelphia when she had felt alone, solitary. Now, cocooned here on the plains, surrounded with new friends as well as Ethan and Jacob and Luther, she realized how much she had needed a family.

"Jacob's ninth birthday is on Thanksgiving Day. Shall we plan a surprise party for him? Redfern, John, and their boys are already coming for dinner."

"You," Ethan countered, "are a continuous wonder. A surprise party on Thanksgiving Day is a fine idea." He reached over and squeezed his wife's leg.

The sun continued to rise, and she was content, but she felt an odd disquiet. Foolishly she looked over her shoulder, telling herself she was being paranoid. Ethan was probably correct that Byron Stanwyck was hundreds of miles away and settling into his new law practice. Still, her serenity had vanished.

Lost in thought, she was almost surprised when Ethan halted the wagon in front of the house. He stepped down and lifted his arms to help her to the ground. She felt the calluses of his palms, the strength of his hands, and the depths of his love. He drew her to his chest and kissed her.

The kiss sent a delicious sensation tumbling through her. She could not imagine life without this man. When he deepened the kiss, her knees went weak. And then she pressed her hands against his chest. "As much as I want you to make love to me, if you don't get this load of lumber to the building site, Luther or Big John or both will come barreling into the yard wondering what's holding you up. It would be embarrassing all around if they were to catch us in the middle of...you know." Heat tinged her cheeks.

Ethan growled in his throat. He kissed her again. "I'll go only if you insist."

She swung away from him, sending a teasing smile. "Then I insist. Tonight Jacob and Luther will have fresh apple pie for dessert, but for you, my handsome husband, I'll have something extra special."

"Woman, you are a temptress." Ethan climbed aboard the wagon, slapped the reins, and turned the horses toward the large gate and down the long lane that led to the main road. He looked over his shoulder and waved. Liberty blew him a kiss.

For no special reason, she lifted her hand to shade her eyes from the sun while looking toward the crosses on the hill a distance from the house. A gust of wind kicked up, sending chills to ripple over her. She quickly sought the warmth and security of the house.

She stoked life into the dying embers in the stove and added kindling to heat it for her pie. Selecting several extra-large apples from the bin, she set to peeling them. She thought about the quilt Redfern was helping her to make for the baby, and the pair of flannel pajamas she was stitching for Jacob's birthday gift, and the special cake she planned to bake for Christmas.

She had blocked all thoughts of Byron Stanwyck from her mind.

Chapter Eight

The stage driver stopped the team in front of the general store. He hopped down from the high seat and opened the door. "Mineola, for you folks who're staying. Thirty minutes for those of you traveling on. Time enough to grab a bite to eat." He pointed to the café.

The town wasn't much—general store, lumber yard, livery stable, two saloons, a church, and a bank, all huddled together on the prairie. Byron Stanwyck grabbed his satchel and followed the small group of travelers across the road. Once inside the small diner, he counted himself fortunate to find an empty seat by the window. He was tired to the bone from the long grueling hours of stagecoach travel from California. He'd finally reached the town he'd thought of so often while still with the wagon train, and a sense of impending reunion lifted his spirits.

"Breakfast special is steak and eggs. Flapjacks extra, if you want 'em." The waitress's tinny voice startled him from his deep thoughts. He had a fire in his belly that had nothing to do with food.

Before he could answer, a wagon drove past. He leaned close to the window. "That woman—who is she?"

The waitress followed his pointing finger. "Why, that's Ethan Wheeler's wife. She's gonna be the teacher for the new country school." She held the pencil ready to write. "Mineola's growing. Yessiree, we're gonna have a town school and a country school. Now, what's it gonna be, mister? I got to get the stagecoach folks fed."

"Coffee and a large slice of apple pie. What's her name?"

"Who? Oh, Mrs. Wheeler. Liberty. Pretty name, ain't it?" She hustled to the next table of waiting customers.

Stanwyck grabbed his satchel and headed to the door. He yelled to the waitress to cancel his order. He hastened down the boardwalk, hoping to spot the wagon. The town was not yet wide awake. Except for a couple of horses tied to hitch rails, and a few buggies, no farm wagons were in sight.

He sauntered back to the café. His stomach reminded him that it had been hours since his last meal. After making a hasty excuse to the waitress, he ordered the breakfast special. While eating, he mulled the news about Libby's hasty marriage. He mentally calculated the number of months, April to October, since the wagon master had banished her from the wagon train. Stanwyck brushed aside a thread of guilt for his role in Liberty's exile. Inwardly smiling, he formulated a plan to make Liberty his, once and for all.

Two hours later, Stanwyck pulled the rented horse and buggy to a halt. He had passed himself off as a textbook salesman who'd heard about the new school, asking directions from the liveryman. He'd also used his wily charm to inquire about the new schoolmarm, saying he'd like to show her the newest mathematics and literature books. He'd added that as a bonus he'd throw in a set of encyclopedias if he made the sale.

He chuckled at the liveryman's gullibility in swallowing the book salesman story hook, line and sinker.

From a small knoll, he watched a lithe woman with hair the color of spun silk hang sheets on a clothesline. For months she had haunted his mind. "Mine. All mine." He spoke only to himself as she gathered the laundry basket and walked into the house.

Making a quick study of the surroundings left him confident that Liberty was alone. He climbed into the buggy and clucked the horse forward, parking in front of the house. Not bothering to knock, he wrapped his hand around the knob and eased open the door.

He didn't know what was sweeter, the enticing pose of her backside jutting outward as she bent to look inside the oven, or the delectable aroma of apple pie that filled the kitchen.

His crotch hardened at the provocative way her fanny swayed back and forth to the tune she hummed. His heart pounded in his throat, and he fought the need to savage her with his desire. "Libby, my dearest Libby."

The oven door slammed. She straightened, her shoulders stiffening. She turned, slowly, her eyes full of panic. "You...how?"

He was having some difficulty not reaching out and filling his hands with her breasts. "Forgive me, Libby. I didn't mean to startle you."

She let out her breath in a somewhat forlorn sigh. "I am not your Libby. I despise that name."

He reveled in the way her hands wrapped protectively around the small round mound nestled beneath her crisp green apron. Flour powdered her cheek, adding to her beauty. He took a step forward. She sidestepped, trying to put the long dining table between them. "I've come for you, and my baby, Libby."

He lost his ability to control his impulse and lunged forward, gripping her by the shoulders, his mouth on hers, fiercely, painfully. He snatched at her blouse, popping buttons that flew off to land on the floor. White-hot desire surged through him.

She filled her fists with his hair and managed to wrench his head backward. She freed one hand and raked her nails down the side of his face. "You monster!" she heaved, scuttling backward. "Your baby died. It's buried in a little box on the hill." Again she wrapped her hands protectively over her stomach. "This is my husband's child. Ethan Wheeler is my baby's father."

Stanwyck cast her a grave look. He used his handkerchief to wipe the blood that trickled down his cheek. His voice hardened. "You know how I feel about liars, Libby."

"I don't know what you mean."

"The little mound you are protecting. It's *my* baby. We both know it."

Her eyes darted toward the door. "Ethan will be home any moment. Leave now and I won't say anything."

It was the calm quality of her voice that caused him to snap. He laughed, a guttural, mocking sound. "Another lie. I know about the lumber you bought this morning, and about the school being built. He's not here. Don't make me angry, Libby. You know what

59

happens when I'm angry."

She swallowed, her mind reeling. "How did you know where to find me?"

He offered a contrite smile. "Mineola is like every other small town, filled with gossips ready to wag their tongues."

He quickly related how he had fooled the stableman into believing he was a textbook salesman. "I asked for directions to the new school. The man blabbed on and on and didn't bat an eye when I asked how to find Mrs. Wheeler, the new schoolteacher."

Tears trickled down her cheek. "You humiliated me in front of the people on the wagon train, you with your beguiling smile, comparing me to Hester in *The Scarlet Letter*. You did everything short of branding an A on me. How dare you!"

Stanwyck made an exasperated sound. "So what's your point?"

Liberty bristled. "If you cared so much about me and your baby, why did you leave me to die?"

The low, even timbre of his voice was somehow more frightening than the chilling glint in his eyes. "You test my patience, Libby."

****

Byron Stanwyck reached toward Liberty. She backed away, his grip ripping the bodice of her dress. More afraid than she'd been in her entire life, she fought to keep the tremor out of her voice. "Surely Jane Ann has given birth by now. You have your own son or daughter. Why do you want me and my baby?"

He huffed a sigh. "Forgive me, Libby. The entire time I was traveling, I swore I wouldn't touch you. I shouldn't have, especially when you're carrying my baby."

She gathered the front of her blouse together. "Why won't you listen?"

He reached for her. She slapped his hand away. "Do not touch me again."

For a moment he studied her. His face twisted into a sneer, and he spoke in a quiet voice, but his words were blunt. "I've placed Jane Ann in an asylum. That weak, sniveling woman produced a stillborn, and a girl, not even a son. She turned into a raving lunatic. Laughing and crying at the same time. She even threatened to ruin me by telling people what I'd done to you. I tried to tell her that you came willingly. There was no force.

"One minute she was a blithering mass of hysteria, and the next she was pleading with me to send her back to her parents in Maryland. The doctor said Jane Ann would never be well enough to bear more children. She's worthless. For her own good, I had to put her away. Don't you see, that's why I've come for you? I was wrong to convince the wagon master to put you off the train. Forgive me. You must. I demand it!"

Her temper snapped, replacing fear, and she spoke through gritted teeth. "You despicable monster! You did your wife a favor. At least she's rid of you." Liberty was shaking like a leaf now. "I'm glad the seed you forcefully implanted in me died."

His fury was all the more frightening. Before she could escape his reach, he backhanded her, splitting her lip. The salty taste of blood filled her mouth. She spit in his face while trying to shove past him.

His hands gripped her wrists, bruising them. He used his strength to lift her on top of the dining table.

There was ugliness in him, and she refused to allow his ugliness to harm her unborn baby. She felt the color drain from her face. Waves of almost forgotten fear washed over her. Fight, she told herself. Don't give in. Don't be weak. Fight! She was building a beautiful life for herself, and she would not allow this man to crumble it into dust.

"Get off Mrs. Wheeler!" River Finnegan grabbed Byron Stanwyck's shoulders and dragged him from Liberty.

She had completely forgotten today was River's reading and writing lesson. The thirteen-year-old was no match for Stanwyck's strength. He shook the boy off and threw him across the room. River landed with a thud against the door, knocking it open.

Liberty cried out, "Go get Ethan. Hurry!"

The boy scrambled from the room. The sound of hooves pounding from the yard filled Liberty with hope. Stay strong, she reminded herself. Sheer determination kept her eyes level.

"Byron, don't do this. It's senseless. My husband will come for you. You must know that."

For a brief second Stanwyck's eyes shifted toward the open door. He grabbed a fistful of her hair as he refocused his eyes on hers. She could only moan; resistance was impossible when he held her so close. He licked the side of her neck. "My God, if you only knew how badly I want you."

"I'll scream, Byron." The words shuddered out of her. "I will scream." She opened her mouth.

He slammed her body against his. Evil glinted in his eyes. "Go ahead. There's no one to hear you except the chickens and a few horses."

In a move that surprised him, Liberty stomped his foot. He yowled a curse and loosened his grip on her hair, but the heel of her shoe caught on the hem of her dress as she tried to make her escape.

With a swift oath, Stanwyck snaked out his fist and clipped her on the chin. "You asked for it. You made me hurt you, Libby." He caught her in his arms before she wilted to the floor.

He marveled at her small nose and high, elegant cheekbones. Her skin was ivory and warm to the touch. He kissed her, desiring to taste more than her lips. "For the sake of my child, don't make me hurt you anymore than necessary, Libby." He lifted her into his arms, and then his movements became brisk as he moved across the room and out the door.

Chapter Nine

Ethan reached down from the new schoolhouse roof to grab the board Big John handed up. The sound of pounding hooves caused him to straighten. He lifted a hand to shade his eyes from the sun. The sight of a brown-and-white pinto stretched in a full run caused Ethan only mild concern. After all, even his Jacob enjoyed a fast gallop on his pony.

He called out, "Isn't your boy River supposed to be with Liberty today?"

Big John frowned. "Yep, why do you ask?"

Before he could respond, the boy's frantic cries sent chills through Ethan. "Mr. Wheeler...Mr. Wheeler!" River was waving his arms as if desperately trying to get Ethan's attention.

"Something's wrong, John." Ethan scrambled down the ladder.

River Finnegan pulled the pinto to a sliding halt. In one leap, he bounded from the horse's back. Big John grabbed his son. "What is it, boy, your ma?"

River's chest heaved in and out as he sucked in a gulp of air. The words whooshed from his mouth. "He's hurting Miss Liberty."

A chill slithered through Ethan to grip like a fist in his stomach. "Who, River?"

The boy gasped. "Don't know. A bad man. He was hitting and shaking her, and then he tried to hurt me.

Miss Liberty said to run get you. I came as fast as I could."

Blood rushing to his head, Ethan couldn't speak for a moment. Ethan remembered the fear in Liberty's eyes when telling him about Byron Stanwyck and how he'd ill-used her.

He faulted himself for not staying with her today. He'd not taken her seriously when she expressed her concern that Stanwyck might find her. Ethan swore under his breath.

Big John looked at the bruise on his son's cheek. He growled, "I don't know who this man is, but I'll break him in two with me bare hands fer hurtin' me boy."

In the heated frenzy of the moment, Ethan hadn't seen Luther and Jacob walk from the creek to join them. "I'm going with you, Ethan." The old man's voice dripped with malice.

Ethan scowled. "Liberty is my wife. This is my fight. God help the man that puts his hands on her." Ethan berated himself for not honoring Liberty's concern. Now her worst nightmare had come true. He was certain Byron Stanwyck had returned.

He belted out, "John, I'd appreciate the loan of your gelding. It'll be faster than one of the wagon horses. Luther, you ride like hell and get the sheriff."

"Yep, sure, take the horse. What you want me to do?" The big Irishman reminded Ethan of a grizzly waiting to attack.

"Take care of your son and mine. I'll come for Jacob as soon as this business is over. Liberty may need Redfern's assistance. I'll let you know." He vaulted onto the gelding's back, gathered the reins, and tried to keep his voice calm as he leaned down to look at his son. "Help River walk his pony home. It'll need cooling down to keep from foundering."

"Yes, sir." The little boy hesitated. "Pa, you ain't gonna get killed, are you?"

His son's tears tugged at Ethan's heart. "Not on your life, son."

"You gonna save Miss Liberty? I mean, I was just gettin' used to havin' her as my mother."

The fist in Ethan's gut tightened. "I will, son. That's a promise. Now, go on. You and River had best get to cooling out his pony. And you mind what Redfern says." Ethan wanted to haul his son into the saddle and hug away the little boy's fears, but time wasn't on his side.

Big John removed his hat and swatted the gelding on the rump. "Do what you have to do, Ethan. None will fault ye for it. Now, get the hell outta here." Ethan gripped the saddle horn to keep the startled animal from jumping out from under him.

The new school sat five miles from the crossroads between the town and the road to Ethan's farm. He reasoned Stanwyck would most likely try to take Liberty away with him, and he hoped a man unfamiliar with the area would take the main road into town and not cut across country. He turned the horse in the direction of his farm.

He leaned forward, urging more speed out of the spunky gelding. A million thoughts raced through his mind. Stanwyck had a pregnant wife. Why would he return for Liberty? Surely it wasn't for money, since Liberty had already established that Stanwyck had stolen what little she had.

Clods of dirt flew from beneath the gelding's hooves. It seemed the horse moved at a snail's pace. Concentrating on speed, it was by only a fraction of his attention that Ethan spotted the buggy barreling toward him. He hauled up on the reins, pulling the horse to one side to keep from colliding with the buggy. The gelding reared against the sudden tautness, nearly unseating Ethan, and it took several minutes to restrain the excited animal and keep it under control.

Ethan's heart lurched into his throat. He barely caught a glimpse of Liberty's body slumped across the driver's lap. The man yelled and snapped the buggy's whip, urging more speed from the horse. Ethan knew this animal. He'd sold it to the liveryman. A gentle animal, it was old, too old to maintain the speed being demanded of it. It was only a matter of time before the aging creature collapsed. This thought brought another rush of fear to Ethan. A dangerous curve loomed a mile ahead. At such a swift pace, the old horse would never be able to maneuver the turn.

Managing to control his own mount, Ethan galloped after the buggy. Thankful for the animal's strength and speed, still he'd lost several precious minutes. Trees whizzed by as Ethan's vision blurred against the wind. He blinked. He was gaining ground. The rented buggy rattled ahead. Ethan's breath caught in his throat as the conveyance entered the curve and one wheel lifted dangerously. A man's voice bellowed out a curse.

Ethan urged his mount next to the buggy. Just a little more speed and he could reach out and grab the leather leaders to slow the heaving animal.

The tip of the whip lashed out to sting Ethan's bare

hand. He automatically jerked away from the pain.

Liberty had righted herself. She screamed, "Ethan!"

Reaching out again, he glanced over his shoulder. Liberty fought with the driver. He'd dropped the whip. Ethan's blood boiled when the man backhanded Liberty and she slumped in the seat. Once again, he reached for the long leather rein. His gelding bumped against the old horse. The slight collision threw the older animal off balance.

Before anyone could react, the curve, the speed of the buggy, and the slapping of the reins demanded more than the old horse could give. The animal stumbled, screaming its pain as its neck folded between its forelegs. The buggy flipped forward, catapulting over the horse.

A body with flailing arms and legs sailed through the air, reminding Ethan of a broken doll when it landed several feet ahead in the road, near a wooded area.

Liberty? Where was she?

Without waiting for his horse to come to a full halt, Ethan leapt from the saddle. "Liberty? My God, answer me!"

Afraid of what he might find, he raced to the toppled vehicle, dropped to his hands and knees, and looked inside. Relief and fear warred for his attention. There was no sign of Liberty. At least she wasn't trapped beneath the buggy's weight.

He stood and looked around. Where was she?

And then he heard it: the sound of water rushing over small rapids. He'd forgotten about the stream that paralleled the road, almost hidden by undergrowth and trees. Maybe she had tumbled into the woods there. A new fear stabbed Ethan. What if she'd landed in the rapidly flowing icy waters?

Another sound drew his attention: wagon wheels and galloping hooves.

Big John pulled the farm wagon to a halt. "Not knowing what ye'd find, I figured you might need some help."

"I'm mighty glad to see you, John. Liberty's not under the buggy. Maybe she rolled into the woods." He pointed toward the crumpled heap in the road. "That's the driver."

Big John nodded his understanding and lumbered toward the body.

Ethan rushed to the side of the road and followed the downhill slope that led to the stream. "Liberty...Liberty, answer me!"

"Ethan...I'm here, Ethan."

He'd gone a few feet when he spotted her. His breath hung in his throat. She sat hugging her knees. Leaves adorned her hair, tears glistened against her bruised cheeks, blood stained the corner of her mouth, and her lip was severely swollen. The bodice of her dress lay ripped to the waist.

The woeful expression on his wife's battered face tore at his heart. She opened her arms at the sound of his voice.

Ethan knelt and cradled her trembling body. "I'm so sorry for not listening to you. Forgive me."

Her hands shook as she struggled to cover her breasts with the torn remnants of her dress.

Ethan kissed her brow. "Was it Stanwyck?"

She sobbed against his shoulder. "Is he...is he alive?"

"I don't know. John is checking on him." Ethan hugged her close. "I'll guarantee you one thing. He'll never hurt you again."

She pulled away to look at her husband. "He committed his wife to an asylum. Their baby died, and he was convinced"—she placed her hands on the little mound of her stomach—"that our baby was his. He wouldn't listen, Ethan. I told him, but—"

He shushed her. "Let's get you home. I'll send John to take Stanwyck to town and return with the doctor."

The sight of Luther and the sheriff greeted them when Ethan walked up the slope and onto the road with Liberty, secure in his arms, holding the remnants of her dress together. Luther shrugged out of his jacket and raced forward to cover the young woman. "Anythin' I can do fer you, ma'am, all you got to do is ask."

Liberty rewarded the old handyman with an ashen smile.

Big John scowled. "Ran that poor ole hoss into the ground, he did. If that devil's neck wasn't already broken"—John made a motion toward Byron Stanwyck's crumpled body—"I'd break it for him. Don't hold no pity for a man who ill uses women, young'ns, and horses."

Liberty spoke against Ethan's shoulder. "He's dead?"

John gave an emphatic look. "Deader'n a door knob."

The sheriff said, "Luther filled me in on the short of it, Ethan. At least the town won't need to bear the cost of a trial." He hawked a wad and spat. "Luther, help me get the body across a saddle."

Big John offered the use of his gelding. "I'll drive Ethan and his missus home. Luther, I'd appreciate it if you would bring my horse when you return from town."

Ethan lifted Liberty into the back of the wagon. "And, Luther, tell the doctor we'll need him as soon as possible." He climbed in beside her.

Liberty sobbed against Ethan's shoulder. "I'm glad he's dead." She pushed away to look into Ethan's face. "Is that terrible of me?"

Ethan enfolded her in his arms. He kissed the top of her head, inhaling the scent of her hair. A new set of emotions beset him—relief that his wife was safe; relief that he didn't have to kill Stanwyck; and fear that the abuse his wife had suffered at the hands of a mad man and the assault her body had suffered from being thrown from a careening buggy might cause her to lose the baby. It was too much, too much to deal with.

He shushed her. "There is nothing terrible about you, my sweet girl. Byron Stanwyck deserved to die."

Big John slapped the reins and turned the wagon toward Ethan's farm. He held the horses at a steady gait. The sun had slipped below the horizon by the time he halted the team in front of Ethan's house.

"I'll unhitch the wagon and feed up yer stock for ye, Ethan. Redfern will ride over in the morning." He chuckled. "As if wild horses could keep her away." The big man grew solemn. "Liberty has become the daughter we never had."

"I'm much obliged to you, John. Pick a fresh horse from the corral to get you home."

Without waiting, Ethan carried Liberty into the house and to the bedroom. He'd settle her first, then clear the broken glass and the overturned chairs in the kitchen. He didn't want any evidence to remind his wife of her harrowing ordeal.

After he was certain she slept, he walked out to the porch. The crosses on the hill stood white against the day's waning light. His jaw flexed with anger. No more, he thought. No more deaths. Hadn't he earned the right to a wife, a new child, a mother for his son, and a happy life? Life was ugly and unfair. Especially in remote places like this. Heart weary, he watched the sun slide beneath the horizon, choking on the turmoil that warred inside him.

She'd crept on silent feet to stand beside him. "Ethan?" She looped her arm through his.

He offered her a tired smile. "You should be in bed."

She took his hand and placed it on her belly. "The baby…"

He didn't want to know the baby had died. Not now. Not ever. The thought caused his heart to ache. "Liberty…I…"

She whispered as she clasped her hands over his. "Wait, just wait a minute."

He loosed a woeful sigh. And then tears flooded his eyes. "It moved."

Liberty's voice cracked with emotion. "Yes, our baby is alive."

Ethan lifted her into his arms. "Glory be!" He wanted to sing, to shout, and to make love to his beautiful wife. Instead he sputtered, "How about a cup of hot tea laced with honey, just the way you like it?"

She stood on tiptoes and kissed his ear. "Tea isn't exactly what I want, but it will do until I'm rested, and then, my husband, it will be you who will need to rest, once I'm finished with you."

Closing his eyes, he let go the breath he'd been holding.

Chapter Ten

The months passed from October into the New Year. Jacob held up the valentine he'd cut out of a piece of red paper. "You think Miss Liberty will like it?"

River Finnegan frowned at his friend. "When are you gonna start calling her 'Ma'?"

"'Cause she ain't said I could, yet. That's why."

"Why don't you just start doing it?"

The redheaded youngster seemed to ponder the question. He shrugged. "Maybe I will, once the baby is born."

"Out!" Redfern gently closed the bedroom door and walked to a kitchen shelf. She scolded, "Jacob, River, go fishing, go look at the new foals, and stay with Luther until I call you. I don't need you under foot."

She cut a stern glance at her husband and to the man pacing back and forth like a nervous cat. "Make yourselves useful. John, bring in some more firewood. Ethan, draw me two large pots of water and set them on the stove. We'll need lots of hot water."

"How much longer, Redfern?" Ethan stopped pacing long enough to grab the pots from Redfern's hands.

"You should know that babies set their own time, Ethan. It could be an hour, or it could be more."

"She's going to be okay, isn't she?"

"Liberty is strong. She isn't as delicate as she looks."

Ethan obeyed. He walked to the sink and pumped the handle of the new pitcher pump he'd installed, filling two large pots and setting them on the burners. He opened the stove's door and inserted several sticks of wood. Then as if searching for something to keep him busy, he set two logs in the fireplace. When finished, he set to pacing again.

Redfern made a shooing motion with her hands. "Take all that pent-up nervousness outside, Ethan. Go tend to that stallion of yours. I'll call you when it's time."

Ethan hesitated. He'd been down this road before. He dreaded hearing the screams of agony and seeing blood-covered sheets. Jamming his fists into his pockets and hunching his shoulders against the cold, he damned himself for lusting after his beautiful wife, planting his seed in her that brought him pleasure but might cause her death.

Long strides took him to the barn. It took a moment for his eyes to adjust to the dim interior. He blew out a breath to calm himself. Spotting his son, Ethan didn't know how much Jacob remembered about his mother's death, how she'd screamed when the dead baby had ripped through her body, and how she'd closed her eyes never to awaken again. The last thing he wanted was to upset the boy.

"Where's River?"

Jacob leaned over the stall door "Helpin' Luther." He gazed at the spindly-legged black foal that nuzzled its mother. His voice was extra serious for a boy who'd celebrated his ninth birthday only a couple of months earlier. "Pa, you reckon if I prayed hard enough, and used proper grammar, that we'd get a girl baby?"

The earnestness on the little boy's face tugged at Ethan's heart. He suppressed a smile. "Let me understand—you'd rather have a little sister than a brother?"

"Well, heck, yeah. Me and River..." Jacob corrected himself. "River and I are already blood brothers. Besides, I think it'd make Miss Liberty happy having a little girl."

Ethan placed an arm around his son and drew him closer. "It'd make her happy if you would call her Mother or Ma. Proper grammar or not, Liberty loves you." His heart swelled with pride. "And boy or girl, you'll make a fine big brother to our baby."

****

Liberty gritted her teeth and twisted the sheet in her hands until her knuckles were white. It seemed the entire lower half of her body had become one massive, throbbing agony. She tensed again, dreading the next thrust of pain. Her cotton nightgown clung to her, transparent with perspiration.

"It hurts, Redfern. Much worse than when...when I miscarried." She panted as if out of breath. "Please tell me nothing is wrong with the baby."

Redfern lifted the blanket, and a slight smile graced her face. "No need to fret. All is well." She sponged Liberty's face with a cool, damp cloth. "It won't be long. I'll get Ethan."

The Shawnee woman raced to the front door and stepped to the porch. "Ethan...Ethan, come now. Your child is about to be born."

"Redfern...hurry!" Liberty braced on her elbows.

Perspiration-damp hair clung to her forehead. The urge to push was building to another crescendo.

Ethan entered on the heels of the Shawnee woman. Redfern lifted the blanket. "One more good push should do it, Liberty."

Liberty reached out and grasped her husband's hands. Her body arched high off the mattress as she clung to him. Her half-groan, half-scream echoed against the walls of the bedroom. The anguish of childbirth peaked, and then there was relief, a sensation of something slipping from her body, followed by the lusty wailing of an infant.

She saw Ethan's steel-blue eyes dart toward the newborn, then to hers, with what seemed a smile of relief and absolute pride.

"You have a daughter, Ethan," Redfern announced as she cut the umbilical cord. She gently cleansed the red, wrinkled body with warm water.

Ethan's strong jaw flexed and then relaxed. His gaze scored Liberty's face. "*We* have a daughter," he corrected.

"Let me see our child." A joyous exhaustion filled Liberty as she lay against the pillow.

Redfern swaddled the infant in a quilt made from bits and pieces of Jacob and Ethan's old shirts and other scrap materials. She was tiny, and perfect, and with a thatch of strawberry blonde hair. Liberty's eyes glistened with happy tears as the newborn's small hand closed around her finger.

"Time for you to go, Ethan." Redfern lifted the little girl from Liberty's arms. "As soon as I get Liberty cleaned up and she rests for a while, you can bring Jacob in to meet his baby sister."

Too weary to go on, Liberty closed her eyes. She felt his lips on hers. "Ethan?"

He met her gaze. "What is it, my sweet girl?"

"What will we name her?"

The light of the bedroom fire flickered over the room. "My mother's name was Gracie. Yours was Lizette. What better way to honor the grandmothers our daughter will never know than by giving her their names?"

Tears stung Liberty's eyes, and she was stricken by the joyous love she felt for her husband. She smiled at the woman who had become her best friend. "I'd like to add Fern, also. Gracie Fern Lizette Wheeler; and we'll call her Fern."

He answered without hesitation, "Perfect. Redfern and John will make wonderful godparents."

Redfern brushed away a rare tear. "You honor us. I am deeply touched."

Ethan bent to place a kiss on Liberty's forehead. He eased from the bed to tiptoe from the room. "Sleep now. I'll check on you later."

****

The next day, an impatient knock sounded at the bedroom door. Liberty invited the person to enter.

A timid face peered around the door. She motioned him forward. "It's okay, Jacob. Come meet your baby sister." She held the sleeping infant against her shoulder.

Jacob timidly approached the side of the bed. Liberty cradled the baby in her arms and pulled the blanket back to reveal the tiny face. "Would you like to hold her?"

"Will she break?" The question was asked with

sincerity.

Liberty's heart caught when she noticed Ethan leaning lazily against the door frame. "Give Liberty your gift, son."

It was then she noticed that Jacob held his hands behind his back. A bashful smile lit his face. He pulled a small red valentine forward and handed it to Liberty. She read it aloud. "To my little sister from her big brother."

Liberty complimented Jacob on his penmanship, with the promise that she would ask Ethan to make a keepsake box for baby Fern to keep all her treasures. "What are you hiding behind your back in the other hand?"

Jacob held a larger red valentine, this one decorated around the edges with white lacy paper. He cleared his throat. "Redfern helped me with the frilly girl stuff." His face glowed pink.

"That's very sweet. I don't think I've ever had a more beautiful valentine card." Liberty reached to accept the red paper heart.

Ethan came and placed a hand on his son's shoulder. "I think it'd mean more if Jacob read it to you."

The youngster cleared his throat. He offered a snaggle-toothed grin. "Ah, shucks." He held the card forward. "Valentine, may I call you Mother?"

Her heart rose in her throat. There was so much Liberty wanted to say, but she couldn't get the words out. Nor could she hold back the tears.

Jacob gave his father an uncomfortable look. "Gosh, Pa, I didn't mean to make her cry. You ain't gonna tan my hide, are you?"

Aren't going to, Liberty mentally corrected with a chuckle. She opened her empty arm. "You've given me the most perfect gift a son could ever give his mother." She squeezed him against her and kissed his cheek. "It'd please me very much if you'd call me—Mother."

Ethan lifted baby Fern from her mother's embrace, instructed Jacob to sit in the rocking chair, and then placed the infant girl in the arms of her big brother. While the little boy admired his sister, Ethan gently sat on the edge of the bed. He beamed with pride. He laced Liberty's fingers with his, the light in his blue eyes a dangerous one like a night light flickering an invitation. He touched his mouth to hers. "I love you, Liberty."

She lightly brushed his knuckles with her lips. A sensation of homecoming that went far beyond the physical raked over her. She reveled in the soothing comfort of the room's silence. Ethan had saved her. He had given her a home, his protection, his good name, a ready-made family, and now, a beautiful daughter. An inward secret part of her knew her life was just beginning.

It was strange how fate had brought them together, thought Liberty. As evil as Byron Stanwyck was, a small part of her was thankful for the day he'd convinced the wagon master to exile her from the wagon train. Without that terrible time in her life, Ethan would never have found her.

No matter how many years of love she and Ethan had together, Liberty intended to cherish them, and to make the most of every precious moment.

She scooted closer to her husband, and he slid an arm around her waist. Looking up at him with all her heart and soul showing, she whispered, "Remember the promise you made on our wedding night?"

Mischief glittered in his eyes. "You mean about making love until we're old and gray?"

She winked and offered a wickedly teasing smile.

Ethan hugged her close. His voice low, he said, "Keep looking at me like that, and I'll have to build another bedroom on the house before the year is out."

Liberty said nothing. She smiled, thinking of all the good years she and Ethan had to build a legacy together.

Isabelle
and the Outlaw

by

Loretta C. Rogers

Dedication

This book is dedicated to all the friends who
sustain me when I falter
and celebrate with me when good news arrives.
And with love and gratitude
to my brother-Lynn and my sister-Connie,
who are my special cheerleaders.

Chapter One

April 2007

What is wrong with me? Even my dog deserted me after I'd rescued him from the pound.

The question rolled around in Isabelle Lander's head as she gazed out the 747's window. Still suffering from her mother's funeral, Isabelle's thoughts turned inward.

You're always too hard on yourself, Izzy. Don't take life so seriously. So you're divorced? I never liked the blockhead anyhow. And so what if you didn't get full tenure at the university?

Isabelle wiped away the tears. Feeling sorry for herself went against her personal code.

She dug the brochure out of her backpack purse and ran her finger across the glossy picture of an ivy-covered English cottage with as much care as if were an ancient scroll unearthed only moments before.

RELAXATION! Screamed the cheaply-printed block letters at the top of the paper designed to look like a post card. STEP BACK IN TIME AND LET YOUR VACATION BEGIN THROUGH THE GARDEN GATE IN BURY, LANCASHIRE, ENGLAND'S PICTURESQUE COUNTRYSIDE.

She was an intelligent person and knew a tacky advertising scheme when she saw one. Naïve she wasn't—even if she had married Andrew Landers, the low-down cheat who had filed for the divorce and then moved in with his bimbo girlfriend.

All the same, the prospects of being "transported back in time" and "relaxation" prodded at something slumbering deep in her heart, behind a bruised ego and a stack of dusty, broken hopes.

Her thoughts were interrupted when the flight attendant's voice came over the PA system: "Please remain seated until the captain turns the seat belt light off. Enjoy your stay in Manchester and thank you for flying Aero-Europe."

****

A few hectic hours later, Isabelle boarded the train to Manchester. She leaned back in her seat and gazed out the window at the passing countryside and imagined the sweet scent of roses, sitting in a garden swing with a book in her hand, and listening to the twitter-tweets of robins.

She sighed and unzipped her backpack, removing an American History book. She opened it to the bookmarked page and ran a finger across the passage she knew almost by heart telling how Raphael Sinclair had been hanged as an outlaw when he was really an undercover agent for the Pinkerton Detective Agency.

Raphael Sinclair. She batted her eyes to keep the tears at bay. *Perhaps you and I are star-crossed. You died because no one came to save you, just as no one spoke up for me to the tenure board.*

****

1870
Yuma, Arizona

Seven outlaws hanged. Raphael Sinclair was the

2

seventh. Just the mention of that name made a chill shiver down the doctor's spine. He'd seen it on enough Wanted posters to spell Sinclair forward and backward.

He mumbled to himself as he finished wrapping the body, "An oxymoron if I ever heard one. Outlaw named Raphael after an angel and with a last name that starts with S-I-N. Almost like a poetic curse was put on him by his mother."

And a curse it was. The hanging had gone badly for Sinclair. Doc reluctantly looked at the white-draped figure. In all his days he'd never seen a man so difficult to put atop a horse and get a noose around his neck. It took the sheriff and four deputies to haul Sinclair into the saddle. And even when the black hood had covered his face and the men were ready to put a whip to his horse, Sinclair struggled and demanded he was innocent, and if they'd wait there was a telegram coming to clear his name.

The telegram never came.

"Hellfire." Doc hated a bad hanging. It made his stomach churn inside just thinking about how the horse had squealed in pain when the whip was set across its rump. How the horse had reared and pawed the air. How Sinclair twisted in the wind with no broken neck to put him out of his misery.

It was an omen. A bad omen.

When it was all done, the deputies had brought Sinclair to the office. They cut the hands free and crossed them over his chest in a reverent manner.

One of the deputies said, "We'll let you remove the black bag from his head, Doc. I ain't one for seeing a man's tongue gawped out and his face frozen in a mask of terror while he gasped his last breath."

3

Doc didn't give the deputies a second glance as they left his office.

Resigned to his task, Doc walked over to the body. He knew the sheriff would be by soon to take the body away for the burial.

Except for the sound of his breathing and the buzzing of bottle flies, the room was quiet. He leaned over the body, hand outstretched to grasp the hood.

Then he saw it.

The definite rise and fall of the white sheet. One thing Winslow P. Wentworth knew in all of his sixty years of doctoring—dead men didn't breathe.

The hairs on the back of Doc's neck rose. His hands itched to remove the hood, but his feet took action instead. He stepped back.

Too late.

The hand shot out from beneath the sheet and clamped around his neck. Doc squealed like a stuck javelina.

A long moment passed and neither man moved, Doc and the infamous gunslinger. In the silence, he heard the man's labored breathing as Sinclair greedily filled his lungs.

A raspy voice croaked, "Get this damned sack off my head."

Doc's hands trembled as he tugged the black hood from the outlaw's head. As if it were offal he tossed the hood across the room where it landed in a trash barrel.

The outlaw swept the sheet from his body. Doc saw the pasty ashen color of death on the man's face. He looked bad. "You coming alive, son?"

Sinclair's words labored from his throat. "Yeah. Didn't you know Raphael was one of God's seven angels who led the dead to the underworld?"

Doc nodded; he was too scared to comment.

"The telegram. Where is the damned telegram?" The words choked from the outlaw, barely discernible.

"No telegram ever came, son. Nobody cleared you."

Sinclair's hand gripped the doctor's throat.

"Don't lie to me." The outlaw's features tightened. "I ain't exactly in the mood."

"I-I wouldn't lie to you. Not at a time like this." Doc's hands clawed the outlaw's, trying to loosen the tension on his throat.

Then a strange thing happened. Sinclair smiled at Doc. "I reckon I'll have to take you with me."

"You...mean...as a hostage?"

"Something like that."

Sinclair quit smiling. His wrists bled, his neck bled, and by all that was holy, thought Doc, his eyes were as cold as two black marbles.

"I'm an old man, Mr. Sinclair. I'd only slow you down. Besides, the sheriff won't hang you again. Not when the hanging went bad."

"Damn straight he won't hang me again. You got a horse?"

"If you'll let go of my throat, I'll doctor those wounds on your neck and wrists."

The outlaw dropped his hand and Doc let out a choked wheeze. The cords of his neck hurt, and he wondered if this was what Sinclair had felt when the noose tightened around his neck.

He watched the outlaw massage his rope-burned throat and then swing his long legs over the side of the table. "I asked you a question—you have a horse...and

5

a gun?"

The hand reached out and grabbed Doc's throat again. Doc struggled. Fear made the blood drain from his face. "Got a horse out back, saddled and ready to go. Gun's in the cabinet." He stretched his arm out to indicate which cabinet. "Over there."

He reasoned with the outlaw. "I won't tell. You must believe me. I don't believe in hanging a man twice. It's an omen, I tell you. It's an omen."

The outlaw pinned Doc with his eyes the same way his hand pinned Doc around the throat. "Give me time to get away. If you don't, I'll come back from the grave and make your life miserable."

"I swear. I'll give you as much time as possible. Now go on. The sheriff will be here soon to get your body, I mean..."

A foot taller than Doc and lean to the bone from years in the saddle, Sinclair dropped his hand from Doc's throat. He pushed off the table and reached for the cabinet where the pistol lay. He tucked it inside his belt and headed to the back door.

There was no reason for Doc to whisper, "Good luck to you, Raphael Sinclair."

"Ain't no such thing as luck, Doc. Just bad coincidences." Sinclair cleared the back door in a dead run. In a single bound he leapt on the startled horse's back and hightailed it toward the mountains.

****

Isabelle felt a gentle nudge on her shoulder and reluctantly opened her eyes.

"Sorry to wake you, Miss, only ten minutes before we arrive in Bury." Isabelle looked up at a smiling porter.

She suppressed a yawn. "I'm more tired than I thought."

As the train slowed, she stuffed the book into her backpack and stood to collect her carry-on from the overhead compartment.

After she'd gathered her luggage, she walked to the front of the train depot and straight to the only waiting taxi.

"Excuse me. I'd like to go to the Garden Gate Cottage." She pulled out the post card. "It's near Gait Burrow Nature Reserve."

The taxi driver nodded his head. He opened the door for Isabelle and she slid into the backseat.

The drive through rolling farm land with its lush green meadows was a vast difference from Arizona's sand, painted mountains, and deserts.

Isabelle marveled at the neat rows of houses with their white picket fences and yards filled with gardens and bursts of colorful flowers.

"Here we are, Miss." The taxi driver pointed his vintage Fiat down a dirt lane and through a grove of trees that formed a tunnel overlapping the road.

He pointed. "There it is. Garden Gate Cottage."

Isabelle turned and looked over her shoulder in the direction they'd come. She noticed they hadn't passed any other houses. "It's a little off the beaten path, isn't it?"

"Just a half mile to the main road, and an easy bicycle ride into the village." He seemed to sense her anxiety. "If it's crime you're worried about, take no worry. We haven't had a murder or a robbery in…oh…twenty or thirty years."

"I'm not worried." Not about to show her concern,

her answer was quick and sharp. After all, she wouldn't be alone. "I was looking for a place where I'd have peace and quiet." She huffed out a sigh. "Looks like I've found it."

She clutched her backpack. Her fingers discreetly sought the outline of her cell phone. Having it gave her a measure of reassurance.

For some reason she felt the need to offer an explanation, even if it did sound ridiculous. "You see, I'm a firm believer in Murphy's Law."

The cabbie glanced over his shoulder. "Must be an American euphemism. What is this Murphy's Law?"

Her voice sounded foolish as she explained. "Murphy's Law means that odd and unexpected things happen to people for no apparent reason. I seem to be one of those people. So, with Murphy's Law, if it's going to happen, whatever it is, it usually happens to me."

The cabbie's hearty chuckle filled the compact car. He wheeled the vehicle up the circular driveway and parked at the end of a stone walkway.

Isabelle's breath caught on a small, sharp gasp. A strange progression of emotions unfolded in her heart. The ivy-covered cottage looked exactly like the picture on the postcard advertisement. "It's beautiful."

A lanky man dressed in blue shorts and a matching shirt pushed his bicycle toward them.

"Good day to you, Orville. Recognized your old Fiat." The man straddled his bicycle.

"Afternoon to you, too, Gordy." The cabbie opened the door for Isabelle. "This is Gordon Brown. He delivers mail to the cottage."

The lanky man reminded her of the storied

schoolmaster Ichabod Crane. A shiver shimmied down her spine. She hoped this wasn't an omen.

Her thoughts were interrupted when the postman said, "Are you Isabelle Landers?"

She offered a smile. "Yes, I am."

He met her gaze. "Elmira said you'd arrive today. She left on the train to Manchester yesterday. Her sister took ill, sudden like. Said for me to tell you she put the key to the cottage under the welcome mat, and for you not to worry. The pantry is fully stocked and there's homemade ginger cookies and fresh-baked bread, too."

Resisting the urge to get back in the cab, Isabelle asked, "How long will Mrs. Thatcher be gone?"

The postman shrugged. "Don't know. Long as it takes would be my guess. Don't mean to be rude, but I've got more deliveries to make." He pushed off on his bicycle and said over his shoulder, "Elmira said there's a spare bicycle in the shed if you don't feel like walking to the village."

A sudden well of nostalgia filled her. She quickly blinked away the tears that sprang up behind her sunglasses.

The cabbie helped Isabelle to the front door with her luggage. He lifted the welcome mat and retrieved the key.

After unlocking and opening the front door, he handed the key to Isabelle. "Shall I go in with you?"

"I'm sure you have more important things to do." She thanked him for driving her to the cottage.

"The telephone is in the kitchen." He reached into his wallet and pulled out a business card. "Ring me at this number if you should need anything."

Isabelle waved good-bye and watched the car

disappear down the long driveway and out to the tree-covered lane.

Once inside the living room, she spotted an envelope with her name scrawled across the front. The envelope sat propped against a vase of pink roses. The scent of roses teased her nose as she lifted out the note and opened it.

Dear Miss Landers,

I apologize for not being here to welcome you. My sister has taken ill. I have made-up the rose room for you...second door at the end of the hall. I am certain you will find the garden and all beyond a magical place.

Elmira Thatcher

Isabelle folded the note and stuck it back inside the envelope. She looked around at the vaulted ceiling with its exposed beams and at the oak flooring and doors. A wood-burning fireplace with a stone chimney graced one wall of the living room.

She had the odd sensation of coming home to a place she had never seen before. The feeling puzzled her and left her feeling at odds with herself. She ambled over to a bookshelf laden with an assortment of photographs. Her eyes were drawn to a stack of scrapbooks and photo albums neatly arranged on a wicker table.

Isabelle sorted through the stack and selected a scrapbook near the bottom of the pile. Forgetting about her rolling suitcase sitting in the middle of the floor, she made herself comfortable on the floral-covered sofa. Somehow, the scrapbook with its worn edges felt familiar to Isabelle. Her fingers hesitated. With a mental shake, she opened the cover and found nothing significantly important.

Settling back, and careful of the aging paper, she turned the page. Centered on the page was a faded photograph of a covered wagon. A man with a rifle in one hand stood holding a team of horses. A woman sat perched on the high seat of the wagon. Isabelle bent forward trying to see their faces. Inscribed below the picture: Robert and wife, Mary Thatcher Sinclair, Cave Creek, Arizona, 1837.

"Cave Creek, why that's only twenty miles from Phoenix," mused Isabelle. When she turned the next page, a letter fell onto her lap. With infinite care of the fragile paper, she read:

Dearest Sister,

I rue the day we left England and long to return.

Life is hard in the American West and not the adventure Robert dreamed of. How I've come to hate this barbaric land with its half-naked savages, snakes, and bandits.

I fear for the child growing in my womb. We will spend the winter in a place called Cave Creek, Arizona. Robert says after the babe is borne we will travel to California. I miss you dear sister.

Pray for our safety.

Mary

"Poor woman," Isabelle whispered as she matched the corners of the note to the yellowed areas of old paste. Her curiosity in full bloom, she turned more pages, looking at assortments of dried flowers and antique hankies with hand-tatted corners, none of which interested her. She wanted to know more about Mary

Thatcher Sinclair. She found it on the last page. Again, addressed to Dear Sister.

"I wonder who the sister was. It can't be Mrs. Thatcher, she's too young. Must be an ancestor." She bent over the letter dated July, 1839.

Dearest Sister,

I wish you could meet my son. He looks very much like we Thatchers, with slate-gray eyes and thick mop of unruly black hair. On his first birthday, we christened him Robert, after his father, and Raphael after one of God's angels.

By that which is holy, my son needs all the protection God can give him in this lawless land.

The letter went on to tell about the priests and the monastery, and how Mary still yearned for England.

Isabelle sat back and closed her eyes. What fate had brought her to this cottage? Surely the young baby, Raphael, had no connection to the outlaw in her history book.

Swallowing hard at this, she opened her eyes. "Easy, Isabelle, it's just coincidence, pure and simple. Don't read anything else into it."

Placing the album back in the stack, she made sure it looked undisturbed. It wasn't her business to go about snooping in Mrs. Thatcher's personal belongings.

Gathering her luggage, she decided to find the Rose room, and found the walls were the palest of pinks. A rose-patterned quilt covered a four-poster bed. With no window in the room, evening sunlight spilled in through a set of French doors. An old-fashioned highboy sat in the corner and on top of it a vase of yellow, pink, and red roses.

She lifted a music box that sat next to the lamp on the night stand. She turned it upside down and read aloud, "The Merry Widow Waltz."

"Might as well make myself at home." Her stomach growled, reminding her she hadn't eaten in several hours. After settling her things in the bedroom, Isabelle went to the kitchen, where she found a cookie jar filled with ginger snaps. Inside the refrigerator was another note. Isabelle smiled as she read the note saying that inside the plastic container was homemade chicken salad and telling her where to find the bread.

After eating a light meal and making sure the kitchen was left spotless, she showered and changed into a pair of sleep shorts and an oversized T-shirt.

At just past eleven, Isabelle yawned and stretched, knowing she'd have no trouble falling to sleep. She opened the French doors and gazed out into the darkness. She stood for a moment inhaling the sweet freshness of the garden. Crickets played their music and frogs croaked their songs. A smile played across her lips as she closed the doors, set the lock, and then climbed into bed.

Turning the key on the bottom of the music box, she relaxed to the melody for a moment before lifting the book about Raphael Sinclair from her backpack. She flipped through the pages until she found a picture of him. He stood tall and lean against the backdrop of an old western town. He held a saddle slung over his back, and a holster rode low on his hip. And his eyes—his eyes looked directly into hers.

Her breath hung in her throat.

She slammed the book shut and set it on the night

stand next to the bed.

The music had stopped playing. She lifted the silver box and once again wound the key. She punched the pillow to plump it up, turned out the lamp, and scooted under the covers.

"I'm more tired than I thought." Although she whispered the words, her voice sounded loud in the room.

A strange sweet joy, as if she'd come home after a long and difficult journey, filled her as rays from the moon filled the room and sleep visited Isabelle. And the tune from the music box played on.

Chapter Two

1870

A storm rumbled over the horizon, shrouding the light from the moon and the stars. Rafe had pushed the old gelding hard, and the winded horse's sides heaved as it sucked air. Its body trembled with exhaustion.

Rafe's throat hurt. He wanted to speak to the animal, to give words of thanks for the gelding's stout heart. When the soreness of his throat closed off the words, he reached forward and patted the animal's sweat-foamed neck.

He'd crossed the mountain into Apache territory and now stood at the perimeter of an Indian encampment.

Outside the camp, he whistled the call of a night bird. An answering call invited him into the circle of light. He would rest and heal at his blood-brother's lodge.

Lodge fires were a welcomed sight. He was as weary as the horse beneath him. Sliding from the saddle, his legs buckled. Strong arms caught him. He felt himself carried and then laid on a bed of thick hides.

He struggled to keep his eyes open. His throat ached. "Chato, didn't think I'd make it."

Chato squatted by the fire. "You are in a bad way,

my brother."

Rafe winced when the warrior pulled back the shirt and looked at the already festering wounds. "The white man has done this to you?"

He nodded.

Chato made a sound of disgust. "*Wiyan Wakan* will tend to the rope burns on your neck and wrists."

Sturdy hands lifted his head, and a gourd filled with cool liquid soothed his lips. The old woman's voice spoke to him. "Drink deep, *Wasichu*. Sleep will come, white man."

He lay back, exhausted. "Thank you, *Wiyan Wakan*."

The shaman entered the teepee. Sitting cross-legged next to him, he waved a rattle over Rafe's body and chanted in a sing-song voice.

Rafe turned his head and looked into the fire. Bluish-orange flames flickered inside the fire pit. The shaman spoke in a tranquil voice. "It is dangerous out there."

Rafe's eyes shut. He wanted to sleep.

"She is on her way," the shaman said. "She comes to you."

The words pierced his fevered haze. "Who?"

"The woman. She comes from a world very far." With ancient, withered fingers he reached out and plucked at nothing. "She is so close that you might touch her."

Rafe shivered. He put no stock in spells and enchantments and invisible women near enough to touch or otherwise. "Superstition," he managed to say.

In silence he watched the shaman move away into the shadows on feet as silent as a puma stalking prey.

"Don't need a woman. Got to prove I'm innocent," he rasped under his breath while the old woman applied a salve of buffalo tallow mixed with herbs to the wounds, first on his neck then his wrists.

His eyes closed. He thought he heard music—not the raucous sounds from a tinny, out-of-tune piano in a saloon. Rather a melodious tune—a waltz.

Faint memories returned to him—memories he thought he'd lost.

It had been a long time since he'd worn the clothes of a gentleman, or held a genteel woman in his arms and waltzed with her around a room filled with laughter and friends—real friends.

Odd, he thought. The wind must be playing tricks with my mind.

He lifted his head and listened to the voice of a woman, heard the slamming of a door or perhaps the slamming of a book. He must be delusional after his near-death experience.

****

Thunder rumbled and a streak of lightning rent the sky. Isabelle sat up in bed and listened to the ponderous dripping of rain falling off the eaves and pinging against a metal object. She reached over and once more turned the key to the music box.

She settled into her pillows, listening, reaching for memories that eluded her. Her face was wet with tears she couldn't explain. Could the cottage have mystical powers? The notes of the music box surrounded her, caressed her, and finally lulled her back to sleep.

The next morning when she awoke, sunlight spilled through the French doors. She yawned and stretched, and for the first time in a while, she felt refreshed.

After dressing in a pair of tan khaki pants and a short-sleeved shirt, Isabelle leaned over and tied the laces of her tennis shoes in neat bows. She tucked the book about American outlaws and lawmen under her arm and ambled to the kitchen.

She made a pot of tea, buttered two slices of toast, grabbed an apple, and headed back to her bedroom. She opened the French doors and a burst of color greeted her.

With the book tucked under her arm, she stepped out of her room and into paradise.

As a child she'd helped plant flowers in her grandmother's garden and knew many of these flowers by name. Laid out in meticulous patterns were daffodils, white and yellow daisies, foxglove, snowdrops, phlox, and roses—pink, coral, white, and blood red.

Butterflies flittered among the flowers, and the hum of bees drifted in the gentle breeze. As if it had been especially ordered just for her, a tree swing hung from the limb of a sprawling oak tree.

She situated the pot of tea and her cup on a rough hewn table that sat within easy reach of the swing. With her arms draped around stout ropes, Isabelle used her feet to lazily push herself backward and forth, stopping long enough for sips of tea.

Opening the book in her lap, she turned to the page she had bookmarked the night before and read the copy of a newspaper article:

Yuma, Arizona 1870

Proclaiming his innocence, Raphael Sinclair fought with the strength of a mad man. It took Sheriff Ed Brewster and four deputies to lift the outlaw, Sinclair, up on his horse. With his dying breath, Sinclair swore there was a telegram proving his true identity as an undercover detective working for the Pinkerton Agency. No such telegram was ever received clearing Sinclair of his crimes. The deceased's body disappeared the same day of the hanging, with the doctor, Winslow P. Wentworth, declaring that after attending to the six other outlaws hanged with Sinclair, that when he (Doc Wentworth) returned to his office, the body of Sinclair was gone.

"Wow." Isabelle closed the book. "How tragic...how simply barbaric."

She drew a deep breath and shut her eyes for a moment. When she opened them she flipped through the pages to her favorite rendering of Raphael Sinclair.

The reproduction was faded, and with the Stetson he wore pulled low over his forehead, shadows were cast across his face, making it impossible to see his features clearly, though his eyes again seemed to look right at her.

Scanning the pages with the efficiency of a speed-reader, Isabelle searched until she found key words about him—taller than most men...rawboned... piercing eyes...quiet.

Plugging the words into her imagination, she formed her own mental picture of him—including the rope burns on his neck and wrists. The thought of his pain caused her to wince.

A robin's song pulled her mind away from the somber words she'd read. Her eyes followed the bird until it landed high in a thick patch of ivy. The bird's twittering brought a smile to her face.

"Well, aren't you a cheery fellow?"

She turned a page in the book and lowered her eyes to read. In seconds, the robin flew close enough to Isabelle's head that she felt its wing beats.

"My goodness, Mr. Robin Redbreast, if I didn't know better I'd think you were either attacking me or trying to get my attention." She placed her hands over her head and ducked as it swooped again.

The bird flew back to its perch high in the ivy hedge. Isabelle watched it cock its head as if saying, "Look at me."

She laid the book on the wooden table next to the swing. "I know this is positively silly, but, okay…if you insist."

Pushing out of the swing, she walked to the hedge and stood on her tiptoes to look over into the meadow that lay beyond. She spotted a doe with its fawn standing in an apple orchard, helping themselves to fallen fruit. The sight overwhelmed her with joy.

As the animals moved off into the distance, she stretched higher on her tiptoes for a further look. Her foot rolled against a stone, and she lost her balance. She placed her hands against the hedge to steady herself. Her hand touched something cold and round. Fearing she'd touched a snake, she let out a startled shriek and backed away.

Her breath quickened. Little sparks of blue and black danced in front of her eyes. Jet lag, no doubt. She'd take a nap. It was a vacation, after all.

****

Hours later, Isabelle awoke refreshed and ready for adventure. She hummed the "Merry Widow Waltz" as she strolled to the kitchen. She pulled the container of leftover chicken salad from the refrigerator and finished the remains.

With last evening's rain, the afternoon had grown cool. She grabbed a light jacket and headed back outside to the garden.

Scanning the garden, she called, "Where are you Mr. Robin Redbreast?"

She turned in a circle, searching for the little bird. When he didn't appear she decided to explore the meadow. Walking along the hedge, looking for a gate, she grew exasperated. "That's odd, there's no gate."

Tracing a path back toward the cottage, she stopped and turned back to look at the hedge. "I wonder why Mrs. Thatcher doesn't have a gate in the garden. It'd certainly make more sense than walking all the way around to the front of the house to get to the other side."

She placed her hands against her cheeks. "I can't believe it. I'm talking to myself."

When Isabelle turned to walk toward the French doors, the robin twittered. She wagged a finger at the bird. "I've been wondering where you were."

As she faced the bird, the last rays of the sun reflected a glint from beneath the ivy hedge. She walked toward it. Not wanting to reach her hand into an unknown place, she searched the ground for a stick.

Finding one that suited her, she used the sturdy end to push back the thick ivy. Excitement built inside her as she tugged at the growth. "I knew there had to be a gate."

She realized the cold object she'd touched earlier in the day was a large round ring which she supposed was the gate's handle. "I should wait until tomorrow, when there's more light."

Pondering what she should do, Isabelle stood with her hand on the rusted metal ring. Curiosity got the better of her. "One quick peek before I turn in for the night. Then tomorrow, look out. I'm off to explore the countryside."

With the book tucked under her arm, she put her shoulder against the gate and shoved until the wooden structure opened wide enough for her to turn sideways and squeeze through.

She admired the blanket of green that cloaked the hills. Water-ash trees appeared as friendly ghosts along the banks of a creek.

The distant sound of hoof beats drew Isabelle's attention. "Kind of late for fox hunting." She shrugged. "I don't think they fox hunt in England anymore. Probably someone out for an evening ride."

Turning to ease back through the opening, she found the gate missing. She ran her hands along the ivy. "Don't panic. It's here some place."

She tugged at the ivy, forcing it back, only to find another layer of the lush green growth beneath the first. Tamping down panic, she called, "Mr. Robin Redbreast, where are you?" Her voice was firm and loud.

She sighed. "Dammit, bird, this is all your fault."

Her scalp tingled with worry. "Oh, dammit to hell. Murphy's Law. I knew it."

Night had fallen, and the outline of the cottage roof wasn't visible. Sucking in a breath to calm herself, she decided to follow the hedge around to the front of the house and let herself in by the front door. Then she remembered she'd locked the front door and the key was lying on the nightstand next to her bed.

She looked up at the darkened sky and shouted as loud as she could, "Murphy's Law, I hate you." Her voice shattered the night.

A man's voice startled her. He asked in broken English, "Are you in trouble with the law, woman?"

Isabelle's heart raced, and she felt as if she'd jumped completely out of her skin. Her scalp prickled and goose-bumps rippled up and down her arms.

"Holy shit. You scared ten years off…" Her voice faltered. She squinted through the darkness, relieved help had arrived. "Oh, listen, hey. I walked through the garden gate, but now it's closed and I can't find the opening. If you have a flashlight or a lighter, maybe you would walk me to the front door."

When the man didn't answer, she said, "Oh, sorry. My name is Isabelle. Isabelle Landers, I'm…"

"Woman, you talk too much." Strong hands reached down and clamped around her waist. She felt herself lifted and pulled astride a horse's sweaty bare back. She fought the arms that encircled her body.

"Wait just a minute—let me down!" She spoke through gritted teeth as she tried to lift her leg over the horse's neck.

The arms squeezed tighter. "You are in trouble with the law. My brother is in trouble with the law. I take you to him."

"I don't care about your brother, and I'm not in trouble. I'm on vacation."

When the man had kicked the horse into a run, Isabelle was glad to have his strong arms around her. Her butt hurt from the constant pounding, and the sweat from the horse's body caused her to slide sideways.

With each jarring movement, her spine felt as if it were being pushed up between her ears.

"Stop! I demand to know where you're taking me!"

The man behind her remained silent as he urged the horse onward.

"I don't have any money, and there's no one to pay a ransom for me." Her words vibrated as she tried to speak. "Kidnapping is a federal offense. You'll go to prison, you know."

The man behind her said, "You are the one in the shaman's vision."

"I only know a Mr. Gordon Brown. He's a mailman. I don't know a Mr. Shaman." Urgent and fearful, the words rushed from her.

Exhaustion flowed through Isabelle. Still not recovered from jet lag, her eyelids drooped and her chin lolled against her chest. Determined to stay awake, she jerked her head up and stretched her eyes wide. She needed to think, to keep her wits about her. The more she could find out about her kidnapper and where he was taking her, the better she could plan her escape.

"Say, Mister, what's your name?"

He didn't answer.

"Okay. Let's try this again." Enunciating each word, she raised her voice an octave. "What is your name?"

"Your shrieking hurts my ears, woman."

"I have a right to know who is kidnapping me, don't I?" She flung the words at him.

After a few seconds of silence, he said, "Chato."

She was certain jet lag had addled her brain, because she thought she'd heard the man say his name was Chato.

"You mean as in the Apache chief?" Her voice was incredulous.

He answered with a grunt.

Chato? Impossible. He'd died over a hundred years ago. She squirmed around, trying to see his face. "Listen, buster…"

The Apache warrior hauled back on the reins, and the stallion reared. In the next instant, she felt like a sack of potatoes being dumped on the ground.

Chato leapt from the horse, and when he reached down to grab for her hair, his hand came away empty. In the moonlight he stared, puzzled. "Who scalped you, woman?"

Isabelle held her hands over her short-cropped blonde hair. When he reached out again, she batted his hand away. "I wear my hair short. It's the latest fashion."

She gripped her hands together until the knuckles were white. "Look, Mr. Chato, I still have a little jet lag. I'm sure this is all a bad dream and when I wake up in the morning you'll be gone and I'll be lying in a nice comfortable bed."

I hope was added as a silent prayer.

She released her hands and stuck a finger under the Indian's nose. "I can tell you one thing for sure. I think there's something fishy about Mrs. Thatcher's cottage, and as soon as this nightmare is over, I'm going home, back to Arizona."

The Indian touched her forehead with the heel of his hand. "You must have a fever, woman. You are in Arizona."

Completely flustered, Isabelle stammered, "No. You're wrong. I'm in Bury, Lancashire, England, at

Mrs. Thatcher's cottage."

He grabbed her arm. "I know of no such place. We are here, at my village."

He dragged her along with him across a darkened expanse. The conical outline of a structure loomed before her. She had seen them in textbooks about American Plains Indians. "Uh-oh. Bad dream, bad dream. Come on Isabelle, wake up. There are no teepees in England."

Chapter Three

Isabelle let out a tremulous sigh, fighting the urge to scream out her frustration and fear.

The renegade Apache pulled the teepee's flap to one side and gave her an unceremonious shove through the opening.

"Hold your tongue, woman, or I will cut it out." The knife's blade glinted in the firelight as he drew it from the leather sheath at his waist.

To keep her hands from shaking out of control, she stuffed them inside her pants pockets.

"Shaman, I have brought the one called Woman," Chato said icily.

Her gaze shifted to a wizened old Indian sitting cross-legged on a buffalo rug. He reached over and touched the sleeping man on the shoulder.

"Wake now, *Wasichu*. I have summoned the spirits, and they have brought Far Away Woman to help you."

Rafe opened his eyes. In silence, he watched her standing there in the shadows and wondered if he were going mad. A chill racked over his fevered body. An unnamed fear stirred in the pit of his belly.

The shaman swept a rattle over him and muttered some words. With a slight nod, he indicated that Chato and the old woman should leave the teepee.

"Are you an apparition?" The words strained from

Rafe's lips.

"Wow," she said, with a little too much enthusiasm, "this is some dream, and I'll be glad when I wake up."

He raised one eyebrow, as he watched the bafflement on her face.

"Who are you?" he demanded, his gaze moving over her in an imperious sweep of assessment before swinging back to her face. "And why are you dressed like a man?"

He propped himself up on one elbow, and as he waited for her answer observed her strange mode of dress. The tight pants and tucked-in shirt did little to disguise the lush femininity of her body. Jets of sweet fire shot down to collide hard at the crux of his thighs, taking him by surprise.

He noticed her face flushed a beguiling crimson as she stuttered, "I-Isabelle Landers." She swallowed and pulled her body up straighter. "And I'm supposed to be on vacation—in England. I walked through a gate…"

At her hesitation, he prompted, "What gate?"

She bit her lip and appeared in thought before she blurted, "It seems I've walked through a time portal."

Rafe indulged himself in her delicate fragrance. She smelled of fresh air and honeysuckle, and her honey-toned hair looked like it had been kissed by the sun.

She placed a finger against the dimple in her cheek. "My friend, Dr. Samson, teaches paranormal sciences at the university. I've never put much stock in that sci-fi stuff—that is, until now."

"You're gibberish confounds me, Isabelle Landers. What language is this sci-fi?" *What the hell are time portals and black holes? Either she's insane or I'm delirious.*

"Sit down, Isabelle. It strains my neck to look up at you."

She bent down to rest on her knees. Her gasp reminded him of a trapped mouse. Genuine shock widened her eyes as she gaped at the raw wounds on his neck and wrists.

"Dear God," she breathed. "What happened?" Her mouth pinched into a fine line.

He liked what he saw in her face—the gentle hue of distress upon her cheeks, the slight tremble of her mouth, the way her gaze dropped, then rose again as if she wanted to ask more questions.

"Unfortunate accident." As her almond-shaped eyes quizzically held his, he smiled a mirthless smile. "This word, sci-fi, what is it?"

"Why, time travel and black holes in the universe, of course."

"Bah." He glowered at her, his expression ominous. "I once met a man from a traveling medicine show. He spoke of such nonsense. I believe both of you are loco."

He found himself fascinated with her expressive face, the way emotions came and went.

Isabelle loosed a resigned sigh. "Could you ask your friend Chato to take me back to the gate, please?"

"I don't know what method of divination the shaman used to bring you here, Isabelle Landers. But I will not ask Chato to return you to England until you have helped clear my name."

Weariness settled over him as he lay back against the buffalo rug and closed his eyes.

Deep within, Isabelle knew him. He looked exactly the way the tintype pictures and artist renditions in her textbook on American outlaws portrayed him. She knew more about him than he of her.

Isabelle folded her hands in her lap and smiled winningly at the man. "You're Raphael Sinclair."

His hand shot out and gripped her arm in a painful twist until he'd brought her close to his face. "Spy!" He hissed the word. "I swear by all that is holy, I will not hang again. And you, Spy, will not betray me."

The long muscles on either side of his neck were corded, and a muscle pulsed in his jaw.

"You're h-hurting me," she said in a reedy voice. All concerns about disappearing gates and returning to the security of Mrs. Thatcher's cottage had vanished. The unfortunate and frightening truth was—she didn't have the vaguest idea what was happening to her. Still, it was probably easier to be brave when standing up. And she'd be damned if she let another man treat her like her two-timing ex-husband.

She trembled as she watched Raphael, be he outlaw, undercover detective, apparition, or ghost. She snatched her arm away and stood, backing up to the far side of the teepee.

A strange array of feelings enveloped her. Her stomach clenched when someone touched her. She had thought herself alone with the outlaw until she glanced over her shoulder at the woman's strong brown hand.

"Do not be afraid of *Wasichu*," the old woman said in a soft and soothing voice. "You drink this medicine tea Old Woman made for you, and sleep. You have journeyed far to find *Wasichu*, I think, and you must be tired."

Isabelle accepted a cup of steaming liquid with both hands. The woman's kind words and gentle manner calmed her. "Who is *Wasichu*?" Isabelle tested the foreign word on her tongue.

Old Woman pointed at Rafe, who had lain back on the buffalo rug with one arm flung over his eyes. "*Wasichu*—white man."

"Oh," is all Isabelle could manage. She felt cold and was glad she had worn her jacket. She confided in the woman, "Something strange is happening to me. I think I'm having a nervous breakdown."

The woman tipped Isabelle's hand, guiding the beverage toward her mouth. "Drink."

"What is it?"

"Only a tea. Do not be afraid."

She obeyed. The warm liquid tasted of honey and sweet herbs. A heady sensation filled her. The room seemed to wobble. "I'm losing my mind. Aren't I?"

Old Woman smiled as she reached out and smoothed Isabelle's short hair. "No, little one, you are not *witkowin*—crazy woman," she said. "The shaman has made good magic. Do not worry so much. The shaman has been waiting a long time for you." She offered a toothless smile. "Finish your tea."

She led Isabelle to a pallet of furs. "Tomorrow the sun will warm your heart."

Isabelle was beyond trying to make sense of anything. Now she knew how Alice felt when she tumbled down the rabbit's hole.

"What did the shaman mean when he said he'd been expecting me?"

"The shaman sees things. Sees them in smoke, in the mists that rise from the rivers, and in the toss of the spirit bones."

"What is your name? Surely it isn't Old Woman?"

"I am known as *Wiyan Wakan*. Holy Woman."

"Well," Isabelle said, "that certainly clears things up." She sighed as a blanket settled over her. It felt as if motion had slowed down.

"Good night, *Wiyan Wakan*. I probably won't see you in the morning because, when I wake up, I'll be back where I belong. All of this will have been one extraordinary dream."

The old woman waggled a finger. "That other place is the dream, child. You belong here, with *Wasichu*." She nodded in the direction where Rafe slept. "You were on the lost path, but now you are found and will walk the *wanagi tacaku*—the spirit path."

Isabelle's eyelids fluttered and closed. "If you say so." She smiled, turned onto her side, and nestled deep into the buffalo rugs. The subconscious mind, she reflected just before drifting off, is a marvelous thing, full of magic and mystery.

****

Rafe stirred during the night. His body hummed with desire. He looked over at the sleeping lump on the other side of the fire pit. He needed a woman, and copious amounts of rye whiskey. Although she looked like a boy, with her close-cropped hair and wearing men's clothing, he hadn't missed the tantalizing swell of cleavage visible above the missing button on her shirt.

Chato stepped inside the tent, interrupting Rafe's lecherous thoughts. "You are awake, my brother."

"I don't understand any of this, Chato. The shaman says this woman comes from another world." He used a finger to gingerly test the wound on his throat. "I know of England. It's across the mighty ocean called the Atlantic. My parents came from there to America before I was born. My mother talked often of her homeland. She missed it very much."

Chato handed a book to him. "The woman was holding this when I found her. Can you read the words that look like leaves scattered across snow?"

Rafe pushed to a sitting position. Though his body ached, he felt thankful to be alive. He reverently passed his hand over the front of the book. It had been a long time since he'd held anything of such fine quality.

Tilting the book toward the faint glow of embers, he squinted to focus on the words. "A True History of the Old West: American Outlaws and Lawmen."

After reading the title, he opened the book and read the inscription: "Presented with honor to Isabelle Landers, Associate Professor of American History, University of Phoenix, Phoenix, Arizona."

He looked up at the Apache chief. "It says the year is 2007. How can that be, when this is 1870?"

"Enough of these riddles, my brother. I have brought the woman who yaps like a barking squirrel. Now she is your problem." Like a ghost, Chato disappeared into the darkness.

Rafe used a piece of kindling to light a candle of buffalo tallow. His heart pounded with excitement as he read the title of the book again. He opened it, turning the pages as if they were as delicate as the wings of a moth.

He scanned the index, and the name Raphael Sinclair leapt out at him. Drawing in a sharp breath, he turned to the indicated page. He was surprised to find the page already marked with a strip of paper. His heart pounded as he read the gruesome account of his own hanging. He ran a hand over his three-day growth of beard as he peered closely at the tintype photograph and the artist's rendition of himself.

It had been a long time since he'd seen himself in a mirror. Did he really look like the images on the page?

A perverse curiosity forced him to continue reading the words that described his life. A sense of dread filled him as he turned the last page. He wondered if the final paragraph was the reason why the shaman had brought the woman:

It is thought that by some freak of nature Raphael Sinclair survived the first hanging and that his blood brother, Apache Chief Chato, stole the body. This account seems substantiated when Sinclair was found alive, in a teepee, after Chato's camp was raided by the United States Cavalry. Accounts are varied surrounding Sinclair's death. Some say he was shot while trying to escape. Others state that while still proclaiming himself an undercover agent, he was stood in front of a firing squad. His final words were, "Wait for the telegram. It will prove who I really am." Was the Pinkerton Detective Agency ever notified and asked to verify the employment of Raphael Sinclair? Did a telegram ever arrive at the Yuma telegraph office? These facts remain unknown. At the time of death, Sinclair was thought to be thirty-two years of age.

He closed the book. How old was he now? Quick calculations brought a deadly realization. He was born July 28, 1839. He never celebrated birthdays, never gave the date much thought—until now.

In three months he would celebrate his thirty-second birthday—if he lived that long.

He'd been deep in undercover with the Drawdy gang for three years, living from hand to mouth, always on the run, not daring to go near a telegraph office. Maybe the Pinkertons had forgotten about him...maybe they thought him dead.

****

Isabelle opened her eyes, fully expecting the Raphael Sinclair fantasy to be over, leaving reality swirling in its backwash. Instead, the old woman, *Wiyan Wakan*, knelt next to her bed—which wasn't the one in Mrs. Thatcher's cottage.

Isabelle covered her face with both hands and groaned, "This isn't real. I'm hallucinating."

The old woman laughed, her voice mellow, polished, and resonant. "No E-so-bel. You were doing that before, in that other world. Like I told you last night, what you see around you is what is true."

Even though she was more inclined toward wild hysteria than anything else, Isabelle forced herself to concentrate, focus, to keep her internal balance. "My name is Isabelle Landers," she recited in a determined voice. "I live in Phoenix, Arizona. I was born in 1977, and I have a doctorate degree in American History. I was married..."

"All of that is over and done. Here. You eat. You need your strength to make a match with the likes of *Wasichu*."

Isabelle's appetite seemed unhampered by the situation. Determined not to ask the nature of the food, she accepted a piece of fried flat bread, a bowl of berries, and fried meat, which she hoped wasn't rattlesnake. She sipped the strong but pleasant brew from a crudely carved wooden cup. "What is this?"

"Tea from the white oak bark."

"Where is Mr. Sinclair?" Isabelle stuffed another piece of fried bread into her mouth.

"In the council lodge. I have much work. You stay in teepee. The other women will not take kindly to you—beat you with stick, maybe."

A loud commotion stopped her angry retort. Sinclair burst through the tent flap. He grabbed her by the wrist. "Come on, lady. We've got to hightail it for the mountains."

The urgency in his voice caused her stomach to knot. "Wait! Why the rush?"

"Chato's scouts spotted a patrol of cavalry." He grabbed her book and shoved it at her chest. "I ain't waitin' around to die a second death."

His cold, steely gaze riveted on her. He touched his neck and flashed a cynical smile, revealing strong white teeth.

He leaned toward her. "You ever felt a noose around your neck, lady?" His laugh was rumbling and husky.

Her hand went to her neck. She studied his face and felt fear as she met the same cold, dark eyes that had stared back at her from the pages of her book.

Stumbling to her feet and clasping the book to her chest, she followed him outside. The encampment was a hive of activity. Women and children gathered belongings and ran toward hiding places. Wild whoops from warriors, young and old, filled her ears.

A boy of no more than ten held the reins of two saddled horses. Sinclair lifted her into the saddle of a long-legged pinto. "Can you ride?"

"Yes."

"Can I trust you to follow me?" His smile was both mirthless and threatening.

"Yes." Her fear was a small choking sound in her throat. She watched his eyes narrow dangerously as if offering a challenge.

Giving a satisfied nod, in one fluid motion he leaped onto the back of a black horse. The stallion reared and pawed the air, then seemed to spring into a dead run. Isabelle kicked the pinto into action and followed.

The ride became hilly as they headed west. An experienced rider, she pushed the pinto to stay with the black horse as they climbed into a threshold of granite peaks. The going was difficult, and she had little time to be in awe of her surroundings.

It was dark by the time they stopped. All she could see were the outline of pines, more boulders, and part of the rocky trail ahead, pitted and gouged by the weather. Frightened, she turned accusing eyes to the outlaw, who reached up to help her out of the saddle.

He nudged her shoulder. "C'mon, lady. Get your feet moving."

She stared at his amazingly cold eyes. Her voice sounded braver than she felt. "I need to find a place for some privacy. It's been hours, and I have to go—if you know what I mean?"

He pointed to a large boulder. "Make it quick. The boys will have heard the horses by now. Wouldn't be a good idea for them to catch you with your britches down."

Chapter Four

Isabelle's face paled. A swell of panic hit her as she hurried to squat behind a large boulder.

When she returned, he said, "You know how to cook?"

"Give me a frozen dinner and a microwave and I do pretty fair, but to tell you the truth, right now, I'd settle for a Big Mac, a super-sized order of fries, and a large cola."

"Don't talk gibberish, lady. Speak clear." He grabbed her hand and dragged her along behind him.

"What I mean is I'm not a very good cook. Maybe that's why Andrew divorced me. Or maybe it's because I spent more time working on my doctoral dissertation than I spent with him, or maybe it's because I'm not good in b…" She stopped short of the last word. "At any rate, he left me for a big-boobed, bleached-blonde bimbo. There must be something wrong with me. Even the dog preferred my ex over me. Traitor."

She hadn't realized Raphael had let go of her hand until she tripped over a rock and her feet skidded on the bone-dry earth. She reached out, and he grabbed her hand.

"You'd have let me slide over the cliff, wouldn't you?"

"Saved you, didn't I?" He forced her to continue up the path.

"Geez, where's a cop when you need one?"

"Don't you ever shut up, lady? You could talk the ears off a rattler."

"Rattlesnakes don't have ears." She spat the words at him.

"Fortunate for them."

In the distance, firelight flickered through the pines. They approached it, and she could see the light was from a stone chimney left standing from a cabin that had burned down. She counted six men; Raphael made seven.

Fear ripped through her heart as the men stared at her. One of them licked his lips. The hairs pricked at the back of her neck.

"Well, well, looky what Rafe done brought us." A man with a long, scraggily beard sauntered toward her.

Terrified, she stood like a statue, unable to move.

"She gonna do the cooking, Rafe?" Another man called out from the group.

Raphael's voice, deep and raspy, broke her trance. "She'll cook, Branson, and that's all."

"You know the rules, Rafe. Share and share alike. What's yours is ours." A short, stout man pushed forward. He gave a toothless grin. "And I got me a big appetite."

With beefy hands he clasped both sides of her face and pulled her to him.

"Get your filthy hands off me," Isabelle spat.

When his lips locked on to hers, she placed her hands against his shoulders and brought up her knee with enough force to knock a mule down.

His hands clutched his gonads as he fell to the ground and pulled his knees to his chest. His moans brought a hearty round of guffaws from the other gang members.

She took a step back, but Rafe stopped her flight. With nowhere to run, she twisted out of his hold and shot him a look that should have knocked him dead.

"You've got things to do, woman. Fixin's are over there." He indicated with his head.

"How could I have ever felt sorry for you?" Her nerves stretched to the breaking point. "Why, you're no better than these"—she motioned toward the group of leering men—"animals."

Scarcely a second passed before her hand bristled back and met his cheek in a stinging blow. His head jerked to one side.

A jab of shame pierced Rafe.

He studied her for a second and wondered how the hell he'd come to this. When had he stopped being civilized? Though he wasn't sure why, she infuriated him. Damn!

Anger, loneliness, and uncertainty gripped him. Had the Pinkertons forgotten him? Was he doomed to live out the rest of his years as an outlaw?

No. He'd trust the shaman's magic.

Rafe squinted at Isabelle, at the tangled masses of her hair brushed by the night wind, her chin held high, and the fear in her eyes masked by defiance. *Don't worry, Isabelle Landers. I'll keep you safe until the shaman can find a way to return you to your own time.*

His quiet words were like thunder. "Rules don't say nothin' about a man sharin' his wife." His steely eyes looked into the face of each and every gang member to make his point. "And I ain't sharing."

Amid the grumbles and off-color comments from

the outlaws, Rafe lowered his voice and whispered to Isabelle, "You'll be safe with me. Trust me."

His eyes narrowed as a tall, bald-headed man stepped forward. The look he gave Isabelle froze Rafe's blood.

"I'm Drawdy, leader of this here outfit." He glanced at Rafe, who returned the stare, unflinching.

Drawdy's bald head glistened against the firelight. "Just you remember, Rafe, everybody pulls their weight around here, and that includes your woman."

Rafe's hand spanned her tiny waist. He matched Drawdy's stare. It was a standoff. Neither man relented.

Drawdy's hand seemed to itch for his revolver. He wrapped his palm around the handle. He flicked a glance at Rafe's hand.

A mistake.

Rafe shoved Isabelle aside. He was face to face with the outlaw leader now. He made a low sound in his throat. "Your call, Drawdy."

Drawdy caught Rafe's stare again, and Rafe knew he'd backed the man into a corner.

"Hellfire. Aint worth gettin' killed over no scrawny split-tail." The outlaw leader averted his eyes. His angry red face glowed in the firelight. He blurted out, "You claim she's your woman. That don't mean she gets no special treatment. She'll earn her keep."

He stood with legs apart, thumbs resting easy in his gun belt. He looked at Isabelle's clothes. "I say you kidnapped her off a train. Must be from one of them foreign countries. Don't know of no woman round these parts what dresses like a man."

He walked around her as if sizing her up like a prize mare. "If she's your'n, I say prove it right now,

41

right here." He pointed at the ground. "In front of me and the boys, or by God she belongs to all of us."

Rafe touched her cheek with one hand, then thought better of the action and withdrew it. He felt his heart tighten as the men formed a circle around her. As much as he hated it, he had to continue playing his role to protect her.

"Don't look so scared, wildcat." His eyes were intent and amused as he met her gaze.

Some of the outlaws taunted with catcalls, others flapped their arms up and down and clucked like chickens.

Rafe watched her fear give way to unexpected strength, as she pushed through the circle of men to the outer fringes of firelight. She was almost to the safety of the woods when he caught her.

In a rough, quick motion he swung her into his embrace, then crushed his mouth down on hers. The men hooted and hollered the more she tried to fight. Her fists pushed against his broad chest.

Her head jerked right and left as she tried to avoid the bruising kiss. But she lost the battle. His lips moved forcibly on hers, and he knew his unshaven jaw was scrubbing her soft skin raw wherever there was contact.

Then his tongue lunged into her mouth. She broke his hold by twisting away. In the dim firelight, she stared up at him. He saw her trembling.

His face was devoid of compassion. He had a job to do, to humiliate her and prove his loyalty to the gang, to rip her pride away, her dignity and self-respect. It was a shameful price to pay to convince the gang that she was his, to keep her safe.

The second time he intruded her mouth, Isabelle

had the presence of mind to bite him. She sank her teeth into Rafe's probing tongue. He jerked his head back, and she could see blood on his lip.

The slap was unexpected. The force of it snapped her head backward. His hand snaked out and ripped the buttons from her jacket. The gang members cheered.

"I'll cut your heart out, if you touch me," she whispered, her words like acid before he silenced her with another kiss. Knowing she was going to lose, she released an inward sob.

In her struggle, she heard the arm of her jacket rip. Her legs buckled from beneath her. "What kind of monster are you to do this?" Her words came in small bursts.

He hefted her over his shoulder, his hand clasped tight on her buttocks, and carried her into the darkness. She heard more catcalls, and then the men fell silent. The show was over. They would have to make do with listening.

He dumped her on a bed of pine needles behind the old adobe chimney. The ground was cold, and its chill gave her one last burst of strength. She struggled with him. Finally his hands caught hers and pinned them above her head. He covered her.

He lay there, his tall, lean body heavy upon hers. Her breath came hard and fast as she waited for him to start fumbling with the buttons on her shirt and the zipper on her slacks.

"Scream," he breathed into her ear, shifting his weight and grunting in the process.

Her mind didn't register what he'd said. She waited for the onslaught.

He groaned and shifted his weight again. "Dammit,

woman. I said cry out, moan, whimper," he whispered, his mouth close to her ear. "Do it."

Her eyes flew open. She couldn't see his face. "I don't understand."

He shifted again. His legs lay between her parted thighs. He was as hard as a frozen mackerel, but he hadn't moved to unfasten his pants or tried to loosen hers.

"Dammit to hell, woman! I said whimper."

She whimpered.

Shaken and confused, it didn't take much to be convincing. She heard the men's guffaws beyond the darkness, excited by her submission.

"Again," he groaned, grunting in earnest.

She suddenly understood what he was doing. A sob caught in her throat. Raphael Sinclair was a criminal, a lawless man, sparing her from the worst crime a woman could suffer. She was overwhelmed with gratitude that he would spare her at all.

Unable to deal with her conflicting emotions, she began to weep. He grew louder and more urgent until he finally released a savage sound deep from his chest, and lay over her, silent, waiting to see if their act had been good enough to fool the men.

The only sound was her soft crying. When the men began to talk among themselves, as if nothing out of the ordinary had happened, she was aware of Sinclair's weight. Her back felt like ice, but where his chest covered hers was warm. He breathed heavily. They were so close she could feel his heart beating.

"Why?" she whispered, but he touched her lips, silencing her.

His words were low and harsh. "If you speak of

this, you'll get me killed. Worse than that, you'll get yourself killed."

She nodded, but still she questioned why he'd helped her. Her past heaped up on her, causing the dam on her emotions to burst. First there was the death of her mother, then the degrading divorce, the dog's betrayal, and not getting full tenure at the university, and now, oh, and now, she'd been transported to another century, kidnapped, and saved from the worst possible fate a woman could suffer. It was all more than she could handle.

He was an outlaw showing her charity. Her shoulders shook as the tears flowed. She didn't try to suppress the loud sobs.

He sat up and caught a tear on his calloused finger. Hesitantly, he caressed her cheek. Then he heaved himself to his feet and dragged her with him. He tugged the tail of her shirt out of her slacks, reached for the buttons on her shirt and popped two of them off, exposing the mounds of her breast above her pink push-up bra. "Take off your coat."

She numbly obeyed.

"You still haven't answered why, Mr. Sinclair." The words came between sobs and hiccups.

"Only a gentleman is called Mr. Sinclair. And I'm no gentleman, Isabelle. Call me Rafe."

She hiccupped and answered with a nod. "Why?"

He whispered, "Protect the book, Isabelle. It tells the truth about me."

"You mean you really are a det…" He clamped a hand over her mouth.

Placing his lips close to her ear, she barely heard his whispered, "Yes."

He unbuckled his chaps and opened the fly to his denims. Grimly he pushed her ahead of him. They walked back into the firelight with her looking stunned and ravaged, and him satisfied and dominant. He took his time buttoning his pants and tucking in his shirttail.

Drawdy looked at her disheveled appearance and in a snotty voice said, "Men, welcome the bride. Won't be long and she'll be a merry widow." He slapped his thigh and danced an awkward jig at his joke.

All of the men laughed, except Rafe. "Get to dipping up the beans, lady. My stomach is turned inside out from hunger."

He nudged her with his fist to make his point. He sat on a log and commenced cleaning his pistol.

Hours later, the camp settled down and the outlaws drifted to sleep. She should have expected Rafe would require her to sleep with him. The gang considered her his woman, and it was necessary to keep her from escaping. She drew back from his touch. With unexpected chivalry, he put her next to the chimney where she could garner its heat, his own back to the cold night air. He stuffed the holster between them, shoving it low where he could get to his revolver quickly.

Another hour passed. She listened to his snores. Certain he slept deeply, her hand inched down until her fingers wrapped around the loop of the trigger. She tugged on the gun. A hand clamped on her wrist.

"You go exploring down there, Mrs. Sinclair, and you might grab on to something else that's just as hard as the barrel of my pistol."

It was too dark to see his face. A pain shot through her arm as he twisted her wrist. With a moan, she surrendered her hold and tried to pull her hand from his grip.

He held her hand down between them until she felt his hardness. It singed her palm.

Crying out, she struggled to pull away. He held her close. "You said your husband divorced you. You give him any babies?"

"He didn't want children."

Rafe released a long breath, almost as if he were relieved. Then, being the desperado that he was, he rolled over on his side and went to sleep as quickly as he had awakened.

In the darkness, she recalled his movements, his groans, and finally the deep animal sounds of release. She wondered if he were a good actor or if he had actually fulfilled himself?

He made her feel things she wished she didn't. She cursed him, unable to move beneath the rocklike muscle of his arm.

"Damn you, Rafe Sinclair. And damn you, Murphy's Law." She turned so she could see his craggy features. The deep parentheses inset in his cheeks added to his handsome masculinity. Her body had awakened, making its own demands for satisfaction. Her frustration mounting, she slipped her fingers into his soft, glistening hair, loving the way it felt. And loving him—an outlaw who until now had existed only between the pages of a history book. She uttered a little sobbing chuckle at the irony of it.

With a frustrated sigh, Rafe opened his eyes. "Go to sleep, Isabelle. Tomorrow is a long day."

She decided to appeal to his humanity—if he had any. "I don't belong here, Rafe. If it's money you want to take me back to the garden gate so I can return home, I'll max out both my credit cards to pay you."

He propped on an elbow to see her in the moonlight. He placed a finger over her lips. "The night has ears, Isabelle. Come with me."

Clasping her hand in his and using the moonlight, he led her to a mountain pool. "The men will think we have slipped away for privacy." He cautioned her to speak softly.

He stared up at the starry sky. "I know nothing of the strange things of which you speak—microwaves and big Macs and credit cards. I can only guess the shaman brought you here to save my sorry hide—to somehow change history."

"Why can't you ride to the nearest town and send an email?" She corrected herself. "I mean a telegraph."

"I did." He reached up and touched his neck. "It got me hanged."

She stared at the moonlight shimmering on the pool of water. It seemed a lifetime since she'd had a bath. She felt his gaze on her and looked into his troubled eyes. "Tell me how you came to be undercover in Drawdy's gang. What makes him so important?"

She grew quiet as Rafe talked. "Drawdy robbed a train carrying a shipment of gold bullion headed for the federal mint. The Feds hired the Pinkertons to find Drawdy, and they did. But he wasn't talking."

Rafe stopped long enough to roll a cigarette, taking several long drags before speaking again. "I was in prison for manslaughter. Next thing I knew, Colonel Wright from the Pinkertons was offering me full clemency if I went undercover and acted as an informant to help them locate the gold."

When she didn't say anything, Rafe must have figured she was waiting for more explanation.

"Killed a man"—he spread his hands wide—"with these."

"May I ask why?" Guessing he needed to talk, Isabelle refrained from gasping at his confession.

He looked at her with deadpan eyes. "For raping my wife. When I caught up to him, he called her a filthy squaw."

She heard both sorrow and anger in his voice.

He took another drag on the cigarette. "She was in a bad way when I got home from a hunting trip." He flicked the spent cigarette toward the water. "Before she died, she said there were two of them. She had cut both, one deep on the arm and hand—that's how I knew it was him—and the other man..." Rafe reached over and drew his finger from Isabelle's forehead down over her eye, the corner of her mouth, and to her chin.

A shudder racked through her. "Drawdy?"

He answered her with a nod.

On impulse, she wrapped both arms around him and held him tight. "I'm so sorry, Rafe." She pulled back and, though she couldn't see his eyes, knew they were filled with sadness. "Is that why Chato called you brother?"

He was silent, as if trying to control his emotions, until he finally huffed out, "She was his sister."

A fierce tenderness overtook Isabelle, but something more primitive was taking place in her heart. Tears filled her eyes because the emotion was too huge to contain.

She only meant the kiss to offer comfort. A groan—of protest, of loneliness, of need—rumbled up from somewhere deep in his chest, and Isabelle felt the heat and hardness of him against her thigh.

At first, the kiss was a skirmish, but soon it deepened as their tongues did battle and then mated. Isabelle was lost. Her ex-husband had never made her feel the passion she now felt.

"I promise you, Isabelle, I will keep you safe, and when this is over, I will tell the shaman to send you back to your own time," Rafe gasped, when at last the kiss had ended.

Being a rational woman of the twenty-first century, she didn't believe in love at first sight, yet she knew she loved Raphael Sinclair, and if she couldn't say so in plain words, she would tell him with her body. She pulled his shirt up and slid her hands beneath it to caress the warm, granite-like flesh of his back and ribs. He felt sleek and muscular and dangerous.

Rafe took his time undressing her. He simultaneously used his hands and lips to discover her body. She arched her back, whimpering softly, aware of nothing but the sensations he stirred in her as he stroked and suckled and cherished her.

He kissed her forehead, and whispered to her. "Your body reaches for me," he said. "But what does your mind say, Isabelle Landers? I'll have no woman who does not want to be taken."

Like a person deranged from a fever, she clasped his buttocks, splaying her fingers and urging him to enter her. And as he took her, there in the darkness, to the music of the gurgling pool, he placed his lips over hers so that her cries of pleasure would not be heard beyond the copse of the woods.

After they were spent, he held her with ferocious

protectiveness. "I don't know what spells the shaman cast to bring you to me, but you have placed your own spell on my heart, Isabelle."

****

Isabelle was tired of being treated like a slave during the day and a mistress at night, and the constant running from the law was taking its toll on her. The Old West she'd once enjoyed reading about had now lost its romantic appeal.

While Drawdy and his men held up stagecoaches one after another, Rafe continued to use the excuse of staying hidden to keep the woman from thwarting their plans—even to the point of tying her hands with rawhide and securing them to the horn of her saddle.

It sickened her to hear the outlaws' whoops as they terrorized innocent passengers and robbed them of their belongings, and worse. It was on one such occasion, while she and Rafe sat on their horses, high on a bluff, she said, "I can't take this much longer, Rafe. How can I help you if we never get near a town?"

Tears threatened, but she pressed her fingertips under her eyes until the urge passed. After an inelegant sniffle, she said, "If you truly love me, then please, I want to go home."

She turned her head, stricken. To go back meant losing him.

Rafe's bruised heart fell away and shattered on the hard reality of Isabelle's circumstances. Why was it that the mere sound of her voice sent his emotions into a tailspin?

Unable to bear the pleading in her eyes, he turned his thoughts inward. *She's braver than any woman I've ever known.*

He gazed down at the activity below. Drawdy had made no bones about wanting her, and Rafe knew it was only a matter of time before the outlaw leader sent him on some wild goose chase, demanding Isabelle be left behind.

Rafe had claimed her as his woman. He hadn't meant to fall in love—didn't know when he had—but knew it was time to devise a plan to save her even if it meant his own life.

He reached to turn her toward him. "Isabelle, I…"

She jerked away. "Don't make promises you can't keep."

Chapter Five

Later that evening, the men sat around the campfire while Drawdy divvied up the loot. Dipping out the last of the beans, Isabelle stepped among the outlaws. For meat, they had resorted to rabbit or sage hen, and sometimes no meat at all.

One man whined, "Yar mighty stingy with the servings, girlie. I'll strip your hide if'n I find out you been dippin' more fer yourself and Sinclair." He tipped his head toward where Rafe sat.

Her clothes hung on her skeletal figure. She'd lost weight from the meager amount of food left after she'd fed the men each night. When he reached up and grabbed her breast, all the self-control she had tamped down for these many weeks rose to the surface like vinegar mixed with baking soda.

She gripped the handle of the large iron skillet until her knuckles were white, and with a growl that sounded like an enraged she-bear, she heaved a mighty swing, striking the outlaw on the head and knocking him unconscious.

Her gaze lanced Rafe like a shaft of ice. Dizzy with rage, she ran from the camp. An outstretched leg sent her sprawling headfirst at Drawdy's boots. Before Rafe made a move to help her, Drawdy reached down and grabbed her by the arm, dragging her up against him.

She gagged at his fetid breath. Goaded by his

manner, she clenched her quivering fist and rounded on him, landing a solid blow to his chin. Her eyes stung with the bitter saltiness of unshed tears.

Drawdy's grip remained like a vise on her arm. In the other hand he held his revolver, pointed at her head, his piggish eyes taunting Rafe's half-crouched figure.

"Helluva spit-cat, ain't she, boys?" And though a coughing spasm followed his laughter, he kept the barrel of his Colt .45 against her temple.

"Let her go, Drawdy. You've got no quarrel with the woman." Keeping his hands away from his pistol, Rafe stood to his full height. *Bastard. Harm one hair on her head and I'll...*

He cautioned himself when Drawdy made no move to release her.

"She's got spunk, ain't she?" Rafe's gut-busting laughter proved infectious, setting off loud guffaws among the men and diffusing the tension.

Drawdy licked the side of Isabelle's face. "I mean to have me a taste of this hellcat." He hissed the words, spraying her cheek with drops of spittle.

A tall, lanky man with a scraggily beard who called himself Texas Slim stood. He hitched up his baggy pants. "If we don't get some decent vittles, Drawdy, you won't have 'nuf energy to bed the woman. I say send her to town to buy supplies. Rafe can ride along to make sure she keeps her yap shut."

Isabelle stood as boneless as a scarecrow in the circle of men who all agreed she was the one to send to town. Another man called out, "Yeah, she's a stranger to these parts. Ain't no Wanted posters on her."

The ensuing silence was thunderous. Although the night was cool, perspiration tickled Isabelle's upper lip.

As much as she wanted to look at Rafe, she feared she might betray the idea curling around her brain. Instead she cast a desperate glance at her feet.

Another outlaw called out. "We're waiting, Drawdy. You gonna let Rafe take her to town?"

Rafe stepped out of the shadows. "You realize there's posters on me in every town from here to Mexico."

The response seemed to appease Drawdy. "You'll leave at first light. I figger we're ten miles from Rio Verde."

A young gang member, a boy not quite twenty, blurted out, "Ain't that where you hid the gold from the train you robbed over to Fort McDowell?" He clapped his hands together, gave a yahoo, and danced a little jig. "Boys, I say it's time ole Drawdy here dug up them gold bars and…"

An explosion filled the camp as the Colt .45 bucked in Drawdy's hand.

The words died in the boy's throat as blood wept from the hole in the center of his forehead and he crumpled into a meaningless heap.

Drawdy holstered his pistol. "Boy talks too much."

The outlaws' voices rose up against him. "Yeah, Drawdy. What about that gold? Share 'n' share. Ain't that the creed?"

A fat bandy-legged man pushed through the group. "I was with you when you hit that train ten years back. I'm gettin' tired of waitin'. I ain't young no more, Drawdy. I want my share so I can retire down in Mexico, get me a woman… Hell, get me ten women."

The fat outlaw grew serious. "Cat's outta the bag now, Drawdy. If you don't take us to where you hid the gold, I know a few Apache tricks that'll make you talk."

Isabelle watched the scowl on Drawdy's face deepen to a dark shade of purple. She sensed he knew a rebellion was in the making.

Drawdy pointed a grimy finger toward Rafe and Isabelle. "First light. Use his horse to pack the goods." He pointed down at the lifeless body.

Malice blended with his raspy voice. "I hear the noon train from Fort McDowell has another shipment of gold arriving day after tomorrow. Rafe, you and the girl meet us on the outskirts beyond the water tower."

The fat outlaw pushed his point. "Ain't good 'nuff, Drawdy. Sure, me and the boys here"—he swept out his arms—"we'll stick with you, but after this job, you'll take us to where you buried them gold bars." To make his point, he drew a finger across his neck. "Or else."

Drawdy faded into the shadows. When he returned, he tossed a dress toward Isabelle. "You're a sorry sight, woman. Wear this when you go into town. Later, me and you will celebrate, *by ourselves*."

The emphasis on ourselves and the lecherous look he gave Isabelle sent fingers of fear racing through her. Surely he didn't mean to kill Rafe?

****

The sun hung low above the horizon, searing the clouds with crimson and casting long shadows across the flatland. Isabelle stifled a moan as she shifted her aching buttocks in the saddle.

Ahead lay the town of Rio Verde. Rafe's voice interrupted her thoughts. He was asking her to repeat the message. "You have it memorized?"

Her shoulders lifted with the sigh. "For the

umpteenth time, yes."

"Say it, Isabelle."

Without effort, Isabelle said, "Before going to the general store, I'm to go to the telegraph office and send a wire to Colonel C. L. Wright, Pinkerton Agency, Phoenix, Arizona, saying, 'Drawdy plans a surprise party, Fort McDowell, Thursday two o'clock train. Be on time.' And I'll sign it R.R. Sinclair."

"If all this goes wrong, Isabelle"—he turned in his saddle and pointed toward the high bluffs—"Chato has a hideout in the caves. Find him. Get the shaman to send you back to your own time." His words triggered a puckering sensation in the pit of her stomach.

She gazed at his beautifully chiseled face. She refused to think of life without him.

"I was brought here to change history." Her voice exuded more confidence than she felt. "Nothing will go wrong."

Today was Monday. She prayed Colonel Wright and his agents would arrive at Fort McDowell ahead of Drawdy and his gang.

The light was fading fast now. In the sky, darkening clouds were sweeping over the horizon, driven by a breeze that carried the smell of rain.

By agreement, Rafe would wait on the outskirts of town while she rode in alone. He whispered, "Be careful."

She quelled the desire to reach out and touch him. Digging her heels into the pinto's flank, she held tight to the lead rope attached to the bay horse that would carry the supplies.

Lightning flashed above the horizon as she rode into Rio Verde. The horses snorted nervously as thunder rumbled around them. She turned her eyes toward the sky, her voice mingled with the thunder. "For once, just for once, Murphy, why can't you and your damned law do something good for a change?"

By the time she rode into town, the misting rain had turned into a torrent. Lightning cracked across the sky, again. "Come on," she urged the horses toward the end of the street.

Rain streamed down her face, soaking her hair and the blue gingham dress she wore over her khaki pants and shirt. She blinked away the droplets clinging to her lashes. The wet chill increased her panic until she spotted the sign that read Telegraph Office.

She dismounted and tied the horses to the hitching post. Too tired to step across, she trudged through a mud puddle. Water oozed into her tennis shoes, sloshing up between her toes. Weary legs carried her up the steps and into the building.

Her voice broke and trailed off into silence as she struggled to clear her mind. The tall lanky man standing behind the counter was the spitting image of Gordon Brown, the mailman who delivered Mrs. Thatcher's mail at the cottage in Bury, England. She blinked once, then twice. *I'm hallucinating.*

His voice, distinct and clear, said, "You okay, Miss? You look as if you've seen a ghost."

"Is…is your name Gordon Brown?"

"No, ma'am. George Daily. I'm the telegrapher."

She felt his eyes on her, probably curious about seeing a sopping wet, bedraggled stranger dripping water all over his clean floor and wearing a dress two sizes too large.

"I need to send a telegram." She lifted the hem of

the dress and pulled a coin from her pants pocket. "I've got money." She pushed the dollar toward the man.

"Can you write?"

What kind of question was that? Of course she could write. She hadn't had eight years of college for nothing. Instead she offered a simple smile.

He slid a pad and pencil toward her and watched while she carefully printed the message she'd memorized, adding, Urgent You Reply Within The Hour. "How soon can you send this?"

"Right now—if the line is clear."

Isabelle watched as he keyed the old-fashioned instrument. He offered her a smile. "She's all clear." His finger began a series of taps as he relayed the message to Colonel C. L. Wright.

When he'd finished, she asked, "How long before I get an answer?"

The telegrapher scratched his head. "Can't say for sure."

"Okay if I wait until the rain clears? My..." She searched for the correct terminology. "My man won't like it if I'm gone too long."

"You look froze to the bone. Help yourself to the coffee." He nodded toward a potbelly stove in the corner of the small room.

Not wanting to appear overly anxious, she compelled herself to relax as she sat on a straight-backed chair and sipped the strong brew. Before she'd finished, a rapid series of taps drew her to the counter. She forced her face to remain bland. "Is that my reply?"

The telegrapher nodded as he wrote. Finally, he handed her a yellow slip of paper. Her heart beat a steady staccato as she scanned the message.

My family and I gladly accept the invitation. Two o'clock sharp, Thursday. Wright.

She folded the paper and tucked it down her bosom. As she turned to leave, the telegrapher shouted, "Wait."

Panic stabbed at Isabelle. What if he'd put two and two together deciphering the message? Her heart skipped past a couple of beats. She turned back toward the man. Her voice belied her emotions. "Yes?"

"You forgot your change, ma'am. Telegram's only ten cents."

Would he get suspicious if she didn't take the money? She stretched out her hand and watched him count the change. When he'd finished, she laid five dimes on the counter. "This is for the coffee and a little extra for yourself."

****

Thursday arrived with a vengeance. Isabelle sat on her pinto, situated between Drawdy and Rafe. Exhilaration and fear caused her to tighten her hands around the saddle horn. She had no future with Rafe. Her throat constricted with emotion as she recalled his words the night before.

The moonlight had been enough to see his grave expression. He'd whispered, "I've bedded a lot of women, Isabelle." His words had been heated and quick. "You've done something to my heart. I've got a wanting in me like I've never felt. The first time I looked at you, I knew you were special."

She trembled with the remembering. "God, I wish I had a bed," he'd said. "I wish I could take you like your husband did, civilized, not here on the cold ground."

He laid her back against the blanket, covering her

with his long, hard body, and kissed her as if he would never get enough of the taste of her lips.

"No matter what happens tomorrow, Isabelle, I'll always keep you here." He lifted her hand and placed it over his heart.

Then he'd ask her a strange question. "Did you love your husband?"

"No," she'd choked out shamelessly.

He'd bent his head to give her a frenzied kiss, "Isabelle, I…"

Drawdy interrupted her thoughts when his hand snaked out and snatched the reins from her hands. He wrapped the leather straps around the horn of his saddle. "Just so Rafe, here, don't get no ideas 'bout shootin' me and makin' off with you and the loot."

Her terror mounted. The gang watched the locomotive chugging up the track until it stopped at the water tower. Drawdy checked up and down the row of his band of outlaws. "All right, men, we talked about how we're gonna do this. Speak now or hold your peace."

The men covered their faces with bandanas as their answer. The gang urged their horses forward while the waiting train took on water.

"Get on with it." Drawdy trained his Colt .45 at Rafe's back.

Rafe edged his black horse forward and banged with the butt of his revolver on the door.

"Open wide, fellers, and toss out them bags of gold."

The door slid ajar.

Without pause, a small canvas bag was shoved out through the space, and another, until a large pile lay on the ground. The outlaws released loud, gleeful chuckles when one bag fell open and spilled gold coins. Drawdy lost control of his gang as they leapt from their saddles and stuffed bags of gold inside their shirts.

Drawdy, too, loaded his shirt and saddle bags. Mounting his horse, he leaned over and grabbed Isabelle around the waist and hauled her across his lap. "Got me another prize. The girl's mine."

Rafe sneered. "You wife-killing sonafabitch. The squaw that scarred your face was my wife. Remember her?" He thumbed back the hammer on his revolver. "Isabelle is my woman. Harm one hair on her head and you're a dead man."

In the melee of men trying to mount horses without letting go of the canvas sacks, none of them noticed the doors of the boxcar had opened wider and a firing squad of Winchesters pointed at them, but Rafe did.

A tall, muscular man with red hair and a red handlebar mustache called out, "Pinkerton Detective Agency. Drop the bags, boys. You're all under arrest."

Isabelle squirmed against Drawdy's iron grip. *Why am I quaking and wringing my hands like a simpering coward?*

She lowered her head and clamped her teeth on the hand Drawdy used to imprison her breast.

His painful yowl spooked the horse. Trying to maintain control of the prancing animal and needing to make his escape, he shoved Isabelle from his lap. She landed in a painful heap.

She heard the loud retort of a rifle and, as she stood, saw Drawdy haul back on the reins, blood spread out across his chest.

The horse's hoof struck her across the temple, and

she staggered against the searing pain. Darkness shrouded her, and she thought someone called her name.

It was Rafe screaming, "Isabelle!"

****

Rafe scrubbed his hands over his face and through his hair. For the hundredth time, he looked at the clock on the wall. His thoughts drifted again and again to the nights he had made love to Isabelle under a blanket of stars, the way her eager body molded to his. He remembered her little cries as they soared together and the tears in her eyes at their climax.

Restless to the point of frenzy, he paced the room. What the hell was taking the doctor so long? He looked up as Colonel Wright walked through the door of Fort McDowell's infirmary.

"How's the girl?"

"How the hell should I know?" Rafe slammed his fist into the palm of his hand. "It's been hours, and that quack hasn't so much as poked his head out the door."

Colonel Wright stood a little taller and crossed his arms over his broad chest. Without any bantering, he came straight to the point. "Look, Sinclair, about the hanging in Yuma. That was a mistake."

Rafe rubbed his hand against the rough scar on his neck. "Yeah. What happened to the damned telegraph?"

"It was sent. Lines were down."

"That's a helluva excuse. Now that you've got Drawdy and his gang and the Feds have their gold bullion back, what about my pardon?"

Colonel Wright seemed to have forgotten the leather pouch he held, until that moment. He offered it to Rafe. "It's here. Signed by the territorial governor.

You're a free man."

"And the Wanted posters?"

"We've sent telegrams to sheriffs east and west, north and south of Arizona, ordering every poster pulled and burned, with a statement that a full pardon has been granted to one Raphael Sinclair."

The two men shook hands. "There's also a check for three years' back pay and a little something extra. We figure with all the evidence, you were unjustly imprisoned for killing the man who violated and murdered your wife."

Before leaving, he patted Rafe on the shoulder. "Good luck to you, son."

Impatient to know what was happening with Isabelle, Rafe opened the door to the surgery. The doctor looked up. "You can't come in here."

Rafe growled. "I'm in."

He knelt beside the cot. Isabelle looked like a child lying there with a white sheet drawn up to her chin. A purple lump the size of a hen's egg mounded above her right eye. "It's been hours, Doc. When is she going to wake up?"

The doctor poured himself a stiff drink. Rafe declined one for himself. After slogging down the amber liquid and grimacing at its fiery bite, the doctor said, "There isn't much in the medical books about head injuries, I'm afraid."

A worried frown etched Rafe's face. "She'll be okay when she wakes up, won't she?"

The doctor poured another drink. "Brain is a funny thing. She could be addle-pated as a loon, or she could retain all her faculties, or she…"

"Or she could what?" Rafe grabbed the doctor by

the shirt and hauled him up against the wall. The whiskey glass broke when it tumbled from the doctor's hand.

Stammering, the doctor said, "She's been unconscious for hours. Like as not, she's bound to die."

"Not if I can help it." Rafe scooped Isabelle's lifeless form into his arms and headed toward the door.

The doctor protested. "You take her, and she'll die for sure."

Without answering, Rafe kicked the door open and stepped out into the bright sunlight, gently cradling Isabelle as he mounted and spurred his horse away from the Army post.

****

On either side of him, pale sandstone ledges, sculpted by wind into flowing shapes like the curves of a woman's body, rose into the evening.

Rafe saw the smoke as he neared the top of a rock-strewn ridge and knew he was nearing Chato's stronghold. By the time he'd reached the camp, his mind had weighed and rejected several plans. Pale and quivering, Isabelle stirred and moaned as she lay against his chest. Loving this woman wasn't as simple as running with outlaws.

Curiosity seekers surrounded him as he rode into camp. Chato and Old Woman pushed through the small band of people. Rafe lifted Isabelle into Chato's waiting arms.

Old Woman said, "The shaman awaits you, *Wasichu*." She indicated toward the teepee. "Come."

Chato laid Isabelle on a pallet of furs. He joined Rafe who sat cross-legged in front of the shaman. Rafe's eyes narrowed into slits as he looked into the leathery furrows of the medicine man's face.

The medicine man chanted while he stirred the spirit bones with a bony finger. He lifted the wooden bowl and tossed the bones around before dumping them on a piece of deer hide.

Although impatient, Rafe knew to wait for Apache protocol. The shaman's eyes were grave when he spoke. "Far Away Woman is locked between two worlds. She doesn't know which path to walk. She must choose or die."

Rafe searched the shaman's hooded eyes. He shifted forward. "Though she has filled my heart as none other, Isabelle has also fulfilled her purpose. She has changed my destiny."

He struggled to keep an emotional distance. "Conjure up your strongest medicine and send her through the *wanagi tacaku* to her own time." He made the sign of the arrow to indicate spirit path.

Rafe looked across at Chato. "My brother knows the way. He will lead me."

The shaman brewed a tea using mugwort leaves. He passed his hand over it and breathed in the aroma. "This potion will give Far Away Woman safe travel. Her time in this place will be only a dream."

He lifted the bowl to Old Woman. "*Wiyan Wakan* will speak the words."

Wiyan Wakan indicated Rafe should lift Isabelle's head. As Holy Woman spooned small sips of tea between Isabelle's lips, she chanted a prayer. "Father Darkness, Mother Wind, listen to my plea. Take this soul to meet the morning sun's future beyond our time and through the opening in the wall."

Setting the bowl aside, she admonished Rafe,

"Chato will hold the gate while you place the girl inside. Do not let the gate close on you."

Rafe lifted Isabelle into his arms. A halo of peace surrounded her sleeping figure. "What happens if I choose to stay with her?"

"It is not your time, my son. You will wither. Your bones will turn to ash and scatter in the four winds. The girl will never know you."

The shaman pressed against the teepee, holding the flap aside. "Go now."

"Will I have memory of her, Shaman?" Rafe sighed like a person drowning in despair.

"If you so wish. Heed my warning, *Wasichu*. You are doomed if you do not return to your own time before the sun rises in the east." The shaman blew a dust from the palm of his hand.

The night darkened and the winds howled, and the horses sped across time as winged creatures.

****

Moonlight streamed through the portal as Chato pushed back the ivy and his hands grasped the metal ring. He shoved against the gate. "Hurry, my brother. Our journey is long, and we must beat the sun."

With long strides, Rafe carried Isabelle to the swing. He laid her gently on the ground. Then, using his strong arms, he pulled on the old ropes, breaking them and bringing down the tree branch as well, so the swing lay beside her.

In the breathy wind, he knelt and pressed his lips to hers and filled her lungs with the scent of him. He pressed his body to hers and whispered, "I have to love you enough to let you go. You must stay in your own time, Isabelle. Thank you for coming to me."

He lifted her hand and kissed her palm. "Our paths will cross again. I promise. And when they do, I will never let you go."

"My brother?" Chato's voice was impatient. "It is time. I cannot hold the gate open much longer."

Rafe felt hollow and raw on the inside and bruised on the outside as he placed a last farewell kiss on Isabelle's lips. He sprinted through the gate, and with the agility of a puma he sprang to the back of his black horse. The stallion reared and pawed the air and in one leap disappeared through the portal. Chato's whoop echoed like thunder as he followed.

Chapter Six

Isabelle didn't want the dream to end. She felt his kiss, felt his hard stirring against her thigh. She moaned, wanting more.

"Time to wake up, Ms. Landers." Someone pressed her shoulder. Isabelle reluctantly opened her eyes to a nurse standing ready with a thermometer.

She glanced around at the hospital room and the IV in her arm and gave the elderly woman standing beside the nurse a watery smile. Gordy Brown was there, too.

It took a moment for Isabelle to absorb her surroundings. "Why am I in a hospital?"

Mrs. Thatcher smiled. "Oh, my dear, you gave us quite a fright." She hurried on. "My sister made a quick recovery, and when I arrived home, Gordy was rapping on my front door, calling your name." She twisted her hands together. "Naturally, when you didn't answer we were both concerned."

The room spun when Isabelle tried to sit up. She touched the sizeable lump on her temple. "The last thing I remember was sitting in the swing, reading a book." She rested her head back on the pillow.

"It's my fault," Mrs. Thatcher sputtered. "I forgot to warn you that no one has used the swing for years. I suppose the weather-rotted ropes couldn't bear your weight—not to say that you are..." She sputtered again. "Anyhow, my dear, when the ropes broke, part of the tree limb came tumbling down and knocked you silly."

The nurse poked the thermometer under Isabelle's tongue. "You've suffered a mild concussion. Doctor says you can go home today."

"How long have I been here?"

Gordy Brown spoke up. "We rang up the ambulance. They came straight away, evening before last."

The nurse removed the thermometer. "No fever. You can get dressed, Ms. Landers." She handed Isabelle a prescription. "Get this filled at the apothecary before you leave."

Isabelle tried to make sense of the scribbles. "What's this for?"

The nurse gave a sympathetic smile. "You'll have a bugger of a headache for a few days." Before she left the room, she said, "Most patients who suffer concussions tend to have strange dreams which I'm told seem very real."

****

An hour later, Isabelle sat in the cottage's comfortable living room, sipping tea with Mrs. Thatcher. "Please stop apologizing. It wasn't your fault the swing ropes broke." Holding her cup out for a refill, she said, "I'm the one who should apologize for snooping."

When Mrs. Thatcher's eyes widened, Isabelle hastened on. "You see, I looked at one of your scrapbooks." She pointed to the one on the bottom.

"Oh, my dear, the reason I have them on the coffee table is for my guests to enjoy."

"In that case, may I ask—who was Mary Thatcher Sinclair, and what happened to her?"

Elmira Thatcher's face crinkled into a kindly smile. "Mary Thatcher was a great-aunt four times removed." She pulled another scrapbook from the stack and opened it so Isabelle could read the letter glued to a page. "I can only suppose this was Mary's last letter. As you can see, it says the town of Cave Creek, Arizona, was quarantined with smallpox. It's my guess she died along with her husband and son and a lot of other folk."

Isabelle sighed deeply. She set her cup aside and rested her hands on those of the elderly woman. "This has nothing to do with the accident, please understand."

She glanced around the room. "The cottage is homey and the garden is beautiful." Her headache escalated and Isabelle massaged the sides of her temple. "For some unexplainable reason, I feel an urgent need to return to Phoenix."

"Of course, my dear." Mrs. Thatcher assured Isabelle she understood.

After Isabelle had confirmed her flight, the postman drove her and Mrs. Thatcher to the train station. Isabelle hugged them both, promising to visit again.

****

Night after night, Isabelle dreamed she was riding a horse up a windswept canyon. She felt the chill of lying on the ground and the warmth of a man whose face she couldn't see. He disappeared each time she reached out to embrace him.

Boredom set in after two weeks of being cooped up in her apartment. Her headaches had almost subsided and the bruise on her temple was fading. Deciding to finally unpack her luggage, she searched for her book and, not finding it, supposed she'd left it at the cottage.

"I'm getting a little stir-crazy. Don't think I can stand watching another soap opera." She clicked off the television and walked to the bedroom, where she changed out of shorts and into a pair of khaki pants, a matching shirt, and tennis shoes. She gathered her purse and car keys.

Parking her car in the university's faculty lot, she headed to the History and Social Sciences Building. Her tennis shoes made squishing sounds on the freshly buffed tile floors.

As she rounded a corner, she collided with a rawboned lanky man. The stack of books balanced under his chin thundered to the floor, echoing in the empty halls. "Geez, I'm sorry. Are you hurt?" Isabelle apologized as she hurried to help him retrieve the scattered texts.

He adjusted his wire-rimmed glasses. The parentheses in his cheeks deepened with his smile. "My fault. Should have been looking where I was going." He offered his hand. "I'm filling in for Dr. Samson."

Isabelle's heart pattered. "I've been on vacation. What's happened to Dr. Samson?"

"He suffered a heart attack. Open-heart surgery went well, though." The man shifted the books Isabelle loaded into his arms. "Dr. Samson will be out for a semester. Lucky for me—not so lucky for him."

Offering to help with his load, she said, "I wanted to ask him about time portals—whether such phenomena exist."

A short walk led them to an office marked Department of Paranormal Sciences.

With an apologetic grin, the tall man said, "Mind opening the door?"

He dumped his load of books on the desk and relieved Isabelle of hers. After smoothing the front his black western-cut shirt, he again adjusted his wire-rimmed glasses. "Sorry. I haven't introduced myself. I'm Robert Sinclair, Doctor of Parapsychology."

"Isabelle Landers, Assistant Professor of American History."

He invited her to sit. "To answer your question, Dr. Landers, in theory, time portals do exist. Many people claim to have visited other worlds in other eras. However, we have no concrete proof to substantiate these claims."

Dr. Sinclair removed his glasses, grabbed a tissue from the box at the corner of his desk, and proceeded to clean the lenses, all the time watching Isabelle from under lowered eyelids. "You have a particular interest in going back into time?"

"Umm, no. Just curious." When she stood to leave, he rounded the desk and touched her arm. "Say, my birthday is Saturday. I don't really know anyone on campus. I, ah, was wondering if you like to ride horses?"

Her lone dimple deepened with her smile. "As a matter of fact, I do."

He wanted to touch her, to hold her, to breathe in her scent. He cautioned himself. The time wasn't right. "Excellent. I have a small ranch twenty miles north of Phoenix, in Cave Creek. Tomorrow is Friday. Why not drive out and spend the weekend?"

An exasperated snort escaped her lips as she gripped the doorknob. He placed his hand over hers. "Sorry. That didn't come out right. My adopted grandmother lives in the house with me. She raised me to respect women. What about it? I'd hate to turn thirty-two without someone sharing my birthday cake."

"Okay." She offered her hand, and the two shook as if making a pact.

****

Isabelle rose before dawn. It was much too early to drive to Cave Creek, so she used her time to pack, to pay a few bills, and to linger over a third cup of coffee.

She reminded herself to buy a birthday card and a gift on her way out of town.

Two hours later, she drove through a massive adobe archway with a large wooden sign suspended from a chain: Cave Creek Ranch. R.R. Sinclair, Owner.

A quickening gathered inside her as she parked in front of the adobe ranch house. Hesitant, she stood at the bottom of the veranda steps.

"I've been waiting for you, Isabelle. I'm glad you came." Sinclair stepped through the doorway. "Welcome to my home."

She glanced at the open-beamed ceiling, the oak wood floors, and the fireplace in the corner of the room. "This room seems so familiar to me."

"Perhaps it's déjà vu, Isabelle."

She reached into her purse, pulled out the postcard, and held it toward the man who stood head and shoulders taller than herself.

"I spent a few days of my vacation at Garden Gate Cottage in England." She glanced about. "This room reminds me of the cottage."

Soft steps drew their attention away from the postcard.

"Ah, Grandmother. Allow me to introduce you to Isabelle Landers, Doctor of American History. She's also interested in paranormal phenomena."

It felt as if tiny sparks of electricity jolted Isabelle's fingers when she accepted the elfin woman's deeply tanned hand.

"*Wiyan Wakan.*"

"You speak the language of the Apache, Dr. Landers?"

Isabelle frowned. "I have no idea why I said that." She shrugged her shoulders. "Maybe I read it in a textbook. What does it mean?"

The woman smiled. "It means Holy Woman. You may call me Nora."

"Only if you'll call me Isabelle." Looking over the wizened woman's head, she met the intensity of Sinclair's slate-gray stare. Her pulse danced nervously. Time seemed to freeze, and she thought his eyes smoldered with unspoken secrets.

With a nod, Nora excused herself. "My grandson will show you the gardens and stables while I prepare lunch."

****

Nora watched her adopted grandson lead Isabelle out to the veranda. She smiled. While holding Isabelle's hand, *Wiyan Wakan* had silently willed the strength of earth and sky to flow into Isabelle's spirit.

She removed a jar of honey and sweet herbs from the pantry and set about brewing the tea.

****

Isabelle shaded her eyes against the sun's searing arc. There was little similarity between the cacti garden and the one at Mrs. Thatcher's little English cottage. A brown thrasher perched on the arm of a chair. Tucked away in a shady corner was a rose garden filled with bright red and orange tea roses.

Chattering like old friends, she and Sinclair talked about upcoming classes at the university while they strolled across the yard to the cool interior of the stable. He released a shrill whistle.

A pinto stuck its head over the stall door. Isabelle was again stricken with a sense of familiarity. "He's beautiful. What's his name?" She caressed the white-and-brown silken neck.

"Chato, after a famous Apache chief. He's surefooted and will carry you well on our ride."

Another horse thrust his head forward and nickered. Sinclair stroked the black horse. "This is *Catori*, or Spirit in English. He and I have ridden together a long time."

At the dingling of a bell, Sinclair said, "My grandmother calls. Lunch is ready."

After servings of pulled pork, saffron rice, black beans, and flan, Isabelle declared she'd never eaten so much in her life. Sipping a second cup of tea, she asked about the unusual flavor. "I find it refreshing, nothing like I've ever tasted—not even in England."

"It's my own blend, handed down from many generations and made from the bark of the white oak tree." Nora winked at her grandson.

"I look forward to our ride, Isabelle." Sinclair took her by the elbow with a courtly gesture. "Grandmother can monopolize your time tomorrow, over birthday cake." He returned the older woman's wink.

Isabelle wondered why the exchange of winks bothered her.

After a quick stop in the bathroom, she grabbed her jacket, knowing that as hot as the days were, Arizona nights were often chilly. She met Sinclair in the living room and accepted the hat he offered, then followed him outside to the stable, where a ranch hand held the saddled horses.

"We'll ride to the top."

Her gaze followed where he pointed. "Lead the way." Pleasure rippled through her as his strong hands gripped her waist and lifted her into the saddle.

They galloped the horses across the flatlands and toward the red-rocked peaks. The higher they climbed the more familiar the surroundings seemed to Isabelle. The sun dipped behind the mountains. She allowed the pinto to pick its way up the rocky path. Sounds of gushing water grew louder.

Sinclair motioned for them to stop in a pine grove. She dismounted and followed him to the mountain pool. "I can't help feeling I've been here before, yet I know I haven't."

"Perhaps you were here in another life." He took her hand. "Come, let me show you where a band of outlaws used to hole up."

"Outlaws? Who were they?"

"Louis Drawdy and his gang of misfits."

"Drawdy?" Her eyes lit. "He robbed a gold train and led the Pinkertons a merry chase before getting caught. If I recall correctly, he was hanged along with his gang." She drew in a deep breath. "He picked a beautiful spot as a hideout."

When she leaned against the adobe chimney, the weather-weary structure crumbled. Pulling her away from the mass of falling stones, Sinclair wrapped her in his arms.

A silent voice whispered in her heart and sang

through her blood—Rafe. The scent of him aroused her. This was her dream, yet she was here, now, and it was real.

When she shuddered, he pulled back. "Are you cold?"

She released a shaky laugh. "It felt as if someone just walked across my grave."

"My grandmother's tea sometimes has a strange effect on people."

Isabelle managed a questioning smile.

"I have a gift for you, Isabelle."

"For me? It's your birthday, Robert."

"It's in my saddlebag."

Isabelle perched on a large boulder. She watched him walk toward her. Accepting the book he handed her, she tilted it toward the fading sunlight and read the title aloud: "A True History of the Old West: American Outlaws and Lawmen." She looked up questioningly. "I don't understand."

He sat beside her. Wrapping her hand in his, he brought it to his lips and kissed the knuckles. "Read the inscription."

She opened to the inside page and read, "Presented with honor to Isabelle Landers, Associate Professor of American History, University of Phoenix, July 28."

Her next words were barely a whisper, "All my love, Rafe."

He read the questions in her eyes. "My name is Robert Raphael Sinclair. My friends call me—Rafe."

She buried her face in her hands. "Oh, wow. That conk on the head really did addle-pate me." She touched his arms, his face, and his hair. "I'm hallucinating, aren't I?"

He rested his chin on her head, enclosing her in his arms. "No, Isabelle. I'm real."

"But, how?"

While he held her, he explained what had happened after she'd been struck on the head by the horse's hoof, how he'd begged the shaman to send her back to her own time, and how he'd made it look as if the tree branch had broken and caused her head injury.

"Remember, in the teepee, when you handed me the book?" His eyes beseeched her to believe him. "I've kept it all these years and vowed I'd find a way to come to you." His voice faltered. "Will you have me?"

They looked at each other, and the same love that was in Isabelle's eyes was mirrored back from his. He was afraid to hope or believe she could ever really be his.

"Then it wasn't a dream. I really traveled through time?"

He drew her into his arms and whispered, "Yes."

Their lips met in a long, hungry kiss that promised deeper pleasures. "I'll make a fire to keep us warm. It's going to be a long night."

"What about tomorrow, Rafe? Do you have to return to your time?" She hugged him. He was all flesh and bone and steely muscle, and touching him made her weak with longing.

"The shaman made strong medicine. You are now my world." His lips brushed hers, allowing the kiss to deepen until they were both drowning in it.

She felt the tears come. Long fingers of moonlight filtered through the pines. "Welcome home, my love," she whispered against his mouth.

He thought Isabelle looked incredibly beautiful

wearing only streaks of moonlight. He wanted to go slowly, to treat her like the lady he knew she was, but needs hammered at him.

"Don't wait, Rafe. I need you, too."

He drew her close and whispered, "Forever."

McKenna's Woman

by

Loretta C. Rogers

Dedication

To my daughter, Jamie,
who keeps striving to overcome obstacles.

Chapter One

A cloud of gray dust mushroomed upward from the Concord stagecoach's sliding wheels.

"Lord a'mighty, Aunt Sophie. I swear, one of these days Clem is going to run over some poor soul with the way he barrels his team of horses down Front Street." Standing inside the open doorway of the dress shop she owned with her aunt, Audra Tadlock covered her mouth and nose with a handkerchief to keep from choking on the chalky powder that sifted toward her. "And did you see the way Clem had to brace his feet and loop the reins around his elbows to stop the horses?"

The voice of the middle-aged woman who bent over a lady's dress form came muffled through lips full of straight pins. "Shut the door before the dust ruins Mrs. Mercer's new dress."

Casting a beleaguered glance at her aunt, Audra said, "I wish I were taking a trip somewhere." She sighed. "Hopeville must be the most boring town on earth."

Sophie Anderson straightened and rubbed the small of her back. "And we won't get Mrs. Mercer's three new dresses finished before Monday if you stand there wishing your life away."

"Can't we go back, just for a short visit?"

"If you're referring to Bayou George in South Carolina, you know full well the Yankees burned the house and every building down to the ground years ago." Sophie Anderson released an audible sigh as she jabbed pins into the blue muslin fabric. "And the land fell to a bunch of money-grubbing carpetbaggers."

Always curious about strangers who might visit the sleepy town of Hopeville, Texas, Audra lingered in the doorway. She watched the stagecoach door swing wide. Two men stepped down. One, an apparent drummer with a case of samples, dusted himself off and headed toward the saloon. The other was a tall, broad-shouldered man with dark eyes. A fierce, molded strength lay in his tanned, high-boned cheeks. Unruly black hair slid out from the confines of his black Stetson.

Black pants clung to the muscular line of his thighs and ended at the ankle of dusty boots. A bulge beneath his black frockcoat suggested he wore a holstered revolver on his right hip.

Audra flinched when he turned and his eyes met hers. There was a look of hard capability about him. It told her here was a man fully equipped for trouble. Yet as he turned to the stage driver to get his equipment, his movements were indolent.

Sighing to herself, her heart cartwheeled as she reluctantly closed the door to shut out the heat and sand. She grumbled, "I'm already an old maid. When I die, my tombstone will read 'Here lies Audra Tadlock. She died of boredom.' "

Her aunt harrumphed. "Oh, for heaven's sakes, Audra. You're barely twenty. And if you don't help me finish these dresses, you're more likely to die from starvation than boredom."

****

The last of his gear on the ground, McKenna Smith turned to survey the town. The buildings looked as tired as the horses drowsing hipshot at peeling hitching posts. Across the street from the hotel stood the Bank of Hopeville. The ramshackle building listed to one side and reminded McKenna of a ship whose cargo has shifted during a storm.

He called out to a youngster leaning against the red-and-white striped barber pole. "Hey boy, how'd you like to earn a dollar?"

The barefoot lad pasted a grin on his face as he jumped down from the boardwalk. "Gosh, a dollar. What I gotta do, mister?"

McKenna hefted the crate of pewter plates and collodion solution up on his shoulder. He tucked the camera box under his arm. "Carry my valise and that tripod over to the hotel."

"Dollar first, mister."

"Oldest trick in the book, boy. You take my money then run off leaving me to carry my load."

The lad seemed to concentrate on the toe he was scuffing around in the dirt. "You accusing me of being a thief?"

"It's hot, and I'm not in the mood for bantering." McKenna glanced up at the stagecoach driver. "Okay to leave the rest of my gear here 'til I haul this load over to the hotel?"

The grizzled driver shot a pinched frown at the youngster. "Get yer tail in gear, Billy. Yer ma can use the money." The driver directed his attention toward McKenna. "His pa was Waco Bill Watts. It's all Billy's ma can do to keep the boy in tow."

"Waco Bill. Yeah, I photographed his hanging last

year." McKenna reached into his pocket and flipped the boy a dollar. "I need an assistant. I'll pay an honest day's wage for an honest day's work, and half goes to your mother. What about it, boy?"

"Name's Billy, and I ain't no boy. I'm thirteen." He picked up the tripod that was longer than he was tall, gripped the handle of the valise, and shuffled toward the hotel with his load.

After settling in his room, McKenna and his new assistant ambled down the hotel stairs and out to the sidewalk. "Meet me at seven sharp in the morning." Before crossing the street, McKenna said, "What's the sheriff like, Billy?"

The boy scrunched his face into a frown. "He's old, fat, and dumb. Cuffed me on the ears onct."

McKenna chuckled. "In the morning—seven sharp."

Billy shrugged his shoulders and raced away.

****

Sheriff Horace Rooks was just as Billy Watts had described—past his prime and with a protruding belly. As for the man's intelligence, McKenna decided to reserve judgment until proven otherwise.

He removed a folded paper from the inside pocket of his coat. "Afternoon, Sheriff. I'm obliged by the Texas Rangers to present this document to you."

The sheriff adjusted a pair of wire-rimmed spectacles on his nose. He held the paper at arm's length and squinted.

"Says here you're an ex-con working under a temporary pardon. So what's your business in Hopeville?"

McKenna clenched his jaw against the lawman's

derisive tone. "I'm here to photograph anyone you take into custody, so their ugly mugs can go on Wanted posters."

"Smith your real name or one of them aliases?"

McKenna sighed with impatience.

The sheriff handed the document back to McKenna. He reared back on the chair legs. "Well, Mr. Smith, don't think I like you mixin' into my business."

"Take your complaint up with Major Tom Orly of the Texas Rangers." McKenna offered a challenging stare. "I'll need a building to set up my photography shop. Might as well ply my trade and make a few bucks while I'm here. Got any suggestions, Sheriff?"

The sheriff let the chair legs fall forward with a thud. He rose and hitched his pants over his ample belly. "Empty space next to the dressmaker's shop. Miz Anderson and her niece can use the extra income." He leaned forward, splaying his hands flat on the wooden desk. "They're decent ladies, Mr. Smith. I'd take it mighty personal if you show any disrespect toward them."

McKenna rubbed his aching arm. It'd been several years since Bubba Buchanan had shot him. One day soon he intended to return the favor. "Let's clear up a few things, Sheriff. First, the pardon states that I've paid my dues to society. And second, abusing women isn't my style."

"Ya-huh." The sheriff squinted down at the document. He ran a pudgy finger across a line of words. "Says, '*based upon completion of commitment to aid and assist the State of Texas to the satisfaction of the Governor of Texas, forthwith, a full pardon will be granted.*'"

The sheriff peered over the rims of his spectacles at McKenna. "I read in a book once that leopards don't change their spots, neither. As far as I'm concerned, *Smith*, once an outlaw, always an outlaw. I don't like the idea of you being in my town, but don't seem I have much choice."

McKenna tipped his hat and offered a sardonic smile. Since his release from prison, this wasn't the first time he'd met malice from a lawman. One false move and the governor's pardon wouldn't be worth the paper it was written on. "That's right, Sheriff. You *don't* have a choice."

****

Angry strides carried McKenna down the block toward the dressmaker's shop. He figured Billy Watts was right about the age and portliness of the sheriff, but Rooks didn't strike McKenna as a man of low intelligence.

Impatience clouded McKenna's face. Restlessness stirred his shoulders. He gripped the doorknob and shoved the door open.

He was dumbstruck at the face that greeted him. Hair the color of snow tumbled softly over her shoulders. High cheekbones, and eyes like a spring-fed creek, blue, but almost clear enough to see through.

The front of her yellow dress, with a neckline trimmed in lace, framed her willowy figure. His eyes fell to her tiny waist and narrow hips. Beneath the bodice of her dress was no suggestion of a bosom. His assessment slowly moved back up to study her face. He preferred women with curves, and she was straight as a stick.

The young woman, too, appeared stunned when the

door suddenly opened.

She hesitated for a moment. "May I help you, sir?"

McKenna removed his hat. "The sheriff said the dress shop's owner might be interested in renting out the space next door."

Cautiously, she stepped behind the dress form as if to shield herself from his dark imposing features. "I'm Audra Tadlock. My aunt and I own the space. What line of business are you in, Mister—?"

"McKenna Smith. Everyone calls me McKenna." Wrapped up in the mystique of her eyes, he listened carefully to the cadence of her voice, wondering where he'd heard it before. His mind raced. He was sure they had met, but somehow his memory failed him. Realizing he hadn't answered her question, he said, "I'm a photographer and in need of a place to set up shop."

She flashed him a smile. "What do you photograph, Mr. McKenna?"

"There's no Mister, Miss Tadlock, just McKenna."

Heat flamed her cheeks. "Oh, yes, how silly of me. You did say your last name was Smith." Quickly, she launched into a businesslike posture. "My aunt and I normally charge twenty-five dollars a month for the space. There are living quarters behind the larger area. Will that suffice?"

They stood less than a foot apart. McKenna felt his male response to her nearness. There was an edge to his voice when he spoke. "For that price, I'll have to photograph a lot of babies and ladies in pretty dresses, Miss Tadlock." He reached into his pocket, withdrew a money clip and peeled off the bills.

"Please, call me Audra. And I'd like my aunt and

me to be your first customers." She touched her hair, smoothed the skirt of her dress. "Why are you staring at me? Do I have a smudge on my nose?"

"There's something about you that plays at the edges of my mind. I don't usually forget a face."

The nervousness in her voice was apparent. "I've lived in Hopeville since I was eleven. Aunt Sophie and I never travel, so it isn't likely we've met."

"Forgive my rudeness, Audra. Is tomorrow morning, at nine, too soon for me to photograph you and your aunt?"

Audra stepped behind the counter and opened a metal box. From inside, she removed a key. "Nine is perfect. What else do you take pictures of, McKenna?"

"Outlaws—dead or alive. Hangings, too."

She gasped as she handed him the key. "It's doubtful you'll find any criminals here. Hopeville hasn't had any excitement since Billy Watts tied firecrackers to the tails of some horses last Fourth of July. Nearly scared the poor animals to death."

McKenna situated the Stetson on top of his head. "Billy is my new assistant. Maybe a job will help tame him down a bit."

Turning to leave, he tossed the key up in the air and caught it. "If you'll excuse me, I'd like to settle into my new quarters."

"Wait." Audra moved to a door that connected the two spaces. "Come, let me show you." She stepped through the open doorway. "See, we're neighbors."

She was chattering about how dull Hopeville was and how exciting his life must be with all the traveling he did. McKenna forced a smile. He saw the girl's fertile imagination at work as if conjuring up adventures.

He offered an indulgent smile. "Yeah, neighbors." And he stepped into his temporary quarters.

From inside sources, he already knew that Hopeville's mundane world was about to be shattered.

Chapter Two

McKenna worked inside his makeshift darkroom. Word had spread like wildfire a photographer had set up shop in town. Before noon, Billy Watts announced he hadn't hired on to make squalling babies smile, and that all babies were ugly anyhow.

McKenna hadn't faulted Billy when the boy said, "I'll haul 'quipment for you, but I ain't a-flappin' my arms and jumpin' around like a danged chicken no more." And he'd promptly left the shop, slamming the door behind him.

McKenna opened the face of his watch and checked the time. If Major Orly's information held correct, all hell was about to break loose.

The thought of coming face to face with Pistol Pete Buchanan's son brought an ache to McKenna's left arm. He flexed the fingers that still refused to make a full fist. The corner of his lip winged up into a sneer. "After I put a tidy hole between your eyes, Bubba Buchanan, I'll take your photograph and let people see that big, bad Bubba Buchanan can no longer bray like a jackass over his kills."

McKenna lifted the Colt .45 from his holster and spun the cylinder. Six bullets filled the chambers. Before holstering the pistol, he muttered, "One bullet is all I need."

Rubbing the back of his neck, he rolled his

shoulders to ease the tension and then laid out the remaining daguerreotypes to dry.

A fusillade of shots drew him from the darkroom. The sound of breaking glass had him snatching the door open that separated his space from the dress shop.

Sophie Anderson's face was pale with fear. She pointed toward her niece. "Mr. Smith—"

McKenna yelled, "Get away from the window."

Audra turned to greet him with a smile. "Why? It's just Billy Watts up to another one of his childish pranks." She pressed closer to the window.

McKenna lunged, grabbed her around the waist and spun her to the floor. "Are you daft, girl? Don't you know gunshots from firecrackers?"

She covered her head with her arms when a stray bullet chewed a hole through the shop's closed door.

"Join your aunt behind the counter, and both of you keep your heads down." His voice held the authority of one used to issuing orders.

"Where are you going?" Audra's eyes widened at the chaotic scene outside.

"To get my camera and tripod."

"Where's Billy?"

"Quit."

"Then I'm coming with you. You'll need an assistant."

McKenna let loose a string of expletives. "Hellfire and damnation, I said for you to stay put."

Making a mad dash through the adjoining doors, he grabbed his camera box and tripod. By the time he stepped outside, the outlaws had departed as quickly as they'd come—leaving two of their own dead in the dusty street.

****

Audra cupped both hands over her mouth as she stared into the dead men's lifeless eyes. She swallowed the gorge threatening to spill from her throat. With groping hands, she reached out for support.

"You know how much one of these cost?" McKenna snarled as he shoved Audra's hand from the tripod. He caught the camera before it smashed to the ground.

Trying to regain her equilibrium, Audra stared at him. "I've never seen a dead person."

"Apparently, neither have they." McKenna swept his arm at the gathering crowd. "Look at 'em. Just like ants swarming over a Sunday picnic."

Gathering her tremulous wits, she raked him an assessing glance. "They're morbid...you're morbid."

"Told you before, this is how I make my living." His slow, insolent, almost rude stare made Audra realize how unsettled her stomach felt.

She willed herself to match his sardonic stare. Though he was obviously lacking in proper deportment, she puzzled over her attraction to him. With the coldness in his eyes that seemed to stare right through her, and the quirk of his lips in a mocking grin, Smith might be as dangerous as he looked.

He slid a plate into the camera, bent down, and pulled the heavy black drape over his head and shoulders. Seconds later, he whipped from beneath the cloth. "Am I in your way, Miss Tadlock?"

The sarcasm obvious in his voice, she realized she stood in front of the camera lens. "Not anymore." Wheeling away, she shoved through the gawking crowd.

****

McKenna, always closely tuned to the call of danger, looked through the viewfinder and adjusted the lens, his eyes alight with an eagerness the crowd couldn't see.

Sheriff Rooks huffed forward, his six-gun still gripped in his hand. "You know either of them?"

McKenna removed the wet plate from the camera. "Yeah, Joe Basher and Charley Doolin. Part of Pete Buchanan's gang."

"Pistol Pete Buchanan?"

Without bothering to answer, McKenna turned away.

"Where're you going, Smith?"

"To develop this. If I don't do it while it's wet, it'll be ruined. You got any objections, Sheriff?"

"Think I'll tag along." The stout sheriff's short stride was no match for McKenna's.

Inside the dim interior of the shop, McKenna said, "Stay as long as you like, Sheriff, but I've got work to do."

"How come you know the names of those outlaws?" Rooks paused to look at some of the photographs displayed under a glass case.

"I used to be one myself, remember?"

Rooks' eyes narrowed. "For all I know, you still are."

With a trace of impatience, McKenna said, "Shouldn't you be forming a posse, Sheriff? Wouldn't want to lose the trail of those bank robbers, now would you?"

"Deputy's gettin' one up. Care to join us, Mr. Smith? Could be you'd know right where to lead us."

"If you're accusing me of something, spit it out, Sheriff." McKenna narrowed his gaze, his eyes dark. "But you better be damned sure you're right."

Rooks' beefy jowls quivered at the rebuke. "Best you finish up your business in Hopeville, Mr. Smith. Town don't need your kind hanging about." He strode past McKenna, slamming the door as he left.

****

Sleep eluded McKenna, leaving him staring up at the ceiling. He couldn't shake the image of Audra Tadlock from his mind. She wasn't the kind of woman he'd meet in a saloon, and he believed her when she said she'd lived in Hopeville most of her life. There was an honest innocence about her, a quality that made him uncomfortable.

Restless, he rose to relieve himself at the chamber pot, then padded down to the darkroom. He gathered the stack of daguerreotypes he'd taken earlier. Striking a match, he lit the lamp's wick. Settling on a stool with his back propped against the wall, he riffled through the images until he found one of Audra and her aunt. He held the picture closer to the lamplight. Laying that photograph aside, he placed three single shots of her side by side on the counter and held the lamp closer.

Her eyes appeared colorless in the black-and-white images—almost like looking through glass. He reached over and poured himself a shot of bourbon. He chugged down the fiery liquid and grimaced. "Dammit, Audra Tadlock. Where have we met?"

****

Somewhere between sleep and consciousness, the dream came. McKenna felt the bullets rip through his shoulder, he heard the bones shatter, and, in slow

96

motion, watched himself slumping to the ground.

He shifted on the cot to ease the pain on his left side. As he drifted into a deeper slumber, the braying of a jackass rang in his ears. McKenna groaned. He felt the kick as a boot connected with his ribs and then the rough hands turning him onto his back. A madman with a leering grin and colorless blue eyes stared down at him. "Hot damn! I gotcha, McKenna…I gotcha." And then the crazed fiend pulled the trigger one more time.

Bathed in sweat, McKenna jerked to a sitting position, his breath coming in rapid bursts. Rolling off the cot, he grabbed the ewer from the night stand and poured water over his head.

Allowing his eyes to adjust to the darkness, he paced from the living quarters to the shop's darkened interior. With only moonlight to guide him, his fingers searched the area next to the coal-oil lamp until he touched the box of sulfur matches. After lighting the lamp, McKenna feverishly searched through the stack of daguerreotypes he'd developed earlier in the day until he found the ones of Audra Tadlock once again.

For a moment, the room seemed to close in on him. "Damn it all to hell." He stared into the mystical colorless eyes smiling up at him. "She looks enough like Bubba Buchanan to be his twin." In spite of the heat, he shivered.

Chapter Three

"Coincidence, pure and simple. That's all it is, coincidence." Still held by the shock of surprise and forced to pull his mind away from the fact Audra Tadlock was the mirror image of Bubba Buchanan, McKenna didn't hear the man who entered the shop.

"*Mi Dios, amigo.* Only those *loco en la cabeza* talk to themselves." A tall, slender Mexican wearing a pencil-thin mustache and a goatee pointed toward his head and made a rotating motion with his finger. Humor glinted in his dark eyes.

McKenna's face lit into a grin. "Ortiz! Didn't hear you come in."

"Dangerous for an hombre in our line of business." The Mexican returned McKenna's strong handshake. "What's got you talking to yourself, *amigo*?"

Before McKenna could answer, the door leading from the dress shop opened. Audra whirled in with a basket gripped in one hand and a pot of coffee in the other. "McKenna, I thought you might like a bowl of chicken and dumplings and…"

Her breezy smile vanished at the sight of the Mexican, who wore crisscrossed gun belts across his chest. She hurried to set the coffeepot and basket on the counter. "Please forgive my intrusion. I should have knocked first."

Ortiz swept off his sombrero. He bent low from the

waist in a sweeping bow. "*Señorita*, Miguel Pablo Fernando Ortiz, at your service."

McKenna noted the two bright spots of red that flared on the girl's cheeks. He cast a narrowed glance at the Mexican. "Thank you for the food, Audra. Under different circumstances, I'd invite you to stay, but Ortiz is an old friend, and we have some catching up to do."

She stepped backward toward the door. Her hands fluttered to her cheeks. "Yes, of course. Nice meeting you, Mr. Ortiz."

As soon as she'd disappeared through the door, McKenna gathered the basket and coffeepot. "My quarters are back here." He motioned for the Mexican to follow him. He set the basket of food on the table. "We'll talk in here. Never know how thin the walls between my place and the dress shop are."

Ortiz glanced over his shoulder at the open door. "I think I've seen that girl before. Who is she?"

"Damn. You don't how glad I am to hear you say that." McKenna opened the folder lying on the table. "Thought maybe I was losing my mind." He laid out the photographs of Audra. "Look closely."

Ortiz removed his sombrero and tossed it on the bed. He straddled a chair and then picked up each tintype to examine. "Strange eyes—almost like a *persona muerto*."

McKenna rubbed his left arm. "Yeah, a dead person."

By the look on his face, McKenna knew the Mexican bandito turned Texas Ranger was searching his memory banks. "*Aiyee, Chihuahua, amigo. Pistola* Pete's son?"

McKenna poured two cups of coffee and divided

the steaming chicken and dumplings into two bowls. He straddled his own chair at the table. He nodded as he shoveled food into his mouth.

"You think this is a coincidence the *niños* look alike, or if they are, how you say—" Ortiz seemed to search for the word in English.

"Twins? Don't know, but I'll bet you a month's wage I'll find out if she has a twin brother, and if she knows where he's hiding."

"Then what, *amigo*?"

"Then I'm going to kill Bubba Buchanan, arrest the infamous Pistol Pete, escort him to Major Orly, finish my obligation to the State of Texas, get my full pardon, and then get the hell out of Dodge."

"*Aiyee, Chihuahua.* You better draw a breath, *amigo*, or you gonna die from suffocation." Ortiz belly laughed at his joke.

The two men sat in silence while downing their meal. Finally Ortiz said, "You gotta a plan, McKenna?"

"I'm working on it." McKenna scrubbed a fist under his chin. He reached forward and picked up a photograph of Audra. His mind raced. "Ortiz, my friend, you're going to kidnap her."

The Mexican spewed coffee. Drawing the sleeve of his shirt across his mouth, he asked, "Are you *loco*? Why for am I gonna do that?"

McKenna slanted a brief smile. "Bait. I'm going to use her for bait."

"Major Orly, he no gonna like this, *amigo*."

"No, he won't. That's why we're not going to tell him."

****

Audra snipped the thread. "Finished." She laid the

scissors aside and held up the pink satin dress with a deeper shade of rosettes adorning the neckline. She imagined herself at an elegant ball, and waltzing with McKenna. "Mrs. Mercer will certainly look beautiful when she and her husband attend the Cattlemen's Ball in Dallas." She sighed. "Wish I were going someplace, besides to bed."

Sophie Anderson set her own sewing aside. "If you'd accept that nice Mr. Purdy's proposal, you'd be a banker's wife, and instead of wishing your life away, you might have money to travel."

"He's a clerk. Besides, Hiram Purdy is a milksop." Audra grimaced. "Oh, Aunt Sophie, how could you even suggest such a thing?"

Her aunt lifted her shoulders in a shrug. "Then quit your complaining. It's all we can do to make ends meet." She rose from the hard straight-backed chair. "It's late. We'll iron the dresses tomorrow morning, and you can deliver them before noon." She kissed her niece on the cheek. "And make sure Mrs. Mercer pays you. No credit. Heaven knows, if Cyrus Mercer can afford to traipse off to Dallas, he can certainly afford to pay cash for his wife's new wardrobe."

"Goodnight, Aunt Sophie."

"Aren't you coming up to bed?"

"It's too hot. I think I'll sit out on the back steps for a while." Audra lifted the long hair off the nape of her neck.

Sophie Anderson offered her niece a sympathetic smile. "Someday we'll take a trip. I promise." She patted Audra's shoulder, then turned toward the stairs leading up to their living quarters.

****

Fireflies flickered in the ghostly shadows of the alley. Audra left the shop's back door open and, gathering her skirt, sat down on the top step. Perspiration trickled between her breasts. *If it wasn't nighttime, and if the river wasn't so far away, I'd go for a swim.*

Then an idea struck, and the more she thought about slipping over to the livery stable and taking a cool dip in the waist-deep horse trough, the more she liked it. *Only the horses will know, and they won't tell.* She clasped her hands over her mouth to smother the giggles.

She eased off the steps, careful to avoid the squeaky bottom one. Bent on her adventure, she lifted her skirt and headed down the alley. When pain jarred her jaw, her first thought was that she'd somehow bumped into a wall. The last thing she remembered was someone hefting her over their shoulder.

A shadow in the night, Ortiz flung a blanket over the unconscious girl's body. He adjusted her weight on his shoulder and sprinted toward the waiting donkey cart. "*Aiyee, amigo.* Major Orly, he no gonna like this."

McKenna helped Ortiz settle Audra on the floor of the cart. While Ortiz covered her with straw, McKenna tied the gelding he'd purchased to the rear of the wagon. He set his foot on the wheel, climbed up on the seat, and gathered the reins. "That's for damn sure. But the Major did say to use whatever means available to bring in the Buchanan gang."

"Si, but kidnapping?" The Mexican Ranger scratched beneath his goatee. "I don't think that's what he meant."

"You worry too much." A strange excitement filled

McKenna. "Where you headed, Ortiz?"

"Got a little trouble with renegade Apache raidin' back and forth 'cross the border. Goin' to check on my family, and maybe enforce a little six-gun justice while I'm there."

"Orly know about this?"

Ortiz's white teeth gleamed against the moonlight. "Got warrants tucked safely in the sweatband of my sombrero—*Dead or Alive*."

McKenna clasped the up-stretched hand. "Watch your back, my friend."

"*Si. Vaya con Dios, mi amigo*."

McKenna flapped the reins against the donkey's dusty back at once, angling toward Pete Buchanan's stronghold.

Chapter Four

The trail climbed through a thin stand of timber, reached a knoll, and immediately flattened out. Halting the donkey, McKenna swung down to the ground. He thought about leaving Audra in the cart. Better judgment talked him out of it. He brushed the straw covering her to one side. Making little cooing sounds, she snuggled against him as he lifted her. He didn't know if she was still out cold from Ortiz's clip on the jaw or if she was simply sleeping. Either way, he hoped she remained unconscious for the rest of the night. To make his plan succeed, he had work to do before she awakened.

****

Audra's eyelids fluttered open to a butter-yellow half moon rising out of a bank of clouds low in the west. A wind, cool and sage-scented, ruffled the trees and fluttered over her head. She shivered, closed her eyes, and reached for a blanket that wasn't there.

This wasn't a dream. She came fuzzily half awake. Pain seeped through her semi-consciousness, agony crawled along her scalp, and her bruised jaw set up a torturous throbbing. She forced herself to lie still while waiting for her eyes to adjust to the moon's light. With trembling hands, she reached up to run her fingers through her hair. Her hair—was gone. She frantically felt all around her head for her cherished strands. Who had cut off her hair, and more importantly, why?

She eased up on her elbow and ventured a look at the form next to her. McKenna rolled from his side to his back. He groaned, then mumbled a string of incoherent words. Audra watched the agony that distorted his handsome face.

She wondered why he'd kidnapped her and dismissed every sensible reason that popped into her head. Yesterday she was wishing to escape her mundane, day-to-day routine. How often had Aunt Sophie chastised her for wishing her life away? Now she was kidnapped by a ruthless scoundrel who photographed dead outlaws. How had it happened so quickly? And what would happen next?

Gathering her courage, she inched away from his body. Her imagination ran amok as she thought of all the sordid tales she'd heard about men forcing themselves on a woman. Hurtful childhood memories rose to taunt her. She made up her mind to escape or die trying.

Audra shivered as a brisk wind blew across the thicket. She pushed to her knees and then to her feet, willing them to take flight.

Not knowing where she was or how she'd find her way back to the safety of her aunt's arms, Audra sprinted forward. Her feet were yanked from beneath her. Her arms flailed as she reached out for support only to grab empty space. Air swooshed from her chest as she landed with a thud. A sharp smell of dirt and wind filled her nostrils. The thick, rough rope tied around her ankle scraped against her sensitive skin.

Daylight was beginning to seep over the high-serrated ridges of the rocks gnawing at the horizon.

Scowling, McKenna reached forward to reel in the rope secured around his booted foot, and said in a flat tone, "Going somewhere, Audra?"

She rolled over and sat up, brushing leaves and dirt away from her mouth. She could see McKenna's face in the hazy glow. Indignant, she shot back, "You're an outlaw, a renegade who has no more scruples than…than…"

He gave her a curt nod. "Than what, Audra?"

"Why did you kidnap me? Surely it isn't for ransom. You know the poor state the dress shop is in." She refused to cry. Aunt Sophie had always said to cry was a sign of weakness. She stood up and, gathering her courage and crossing her arms over her chest, tapped a moccasin-clad foot impatiently against the ground. "Well?"

McKenna raked her with a slow, thoughtful gaze that made her stiffen and flush. She was well aware of her shabby, dusty appearance. Why did he have to stare at her so knowingly—as if he knew what she was thinking?

"Where are my clothes, Mr. Smith, and why am I dressed like a boy, and who cut my hair…did *you* cut my hair?" She spoke as if her words were lashed together, her voice rising to a shriek. "Why?"

"Shut up!" he hissed. Those curt words made her shudder with apprehension.

She subsided into silence and wondered miserably what sins she had committed in her life that she should be so punished.

McKenna loosened the noose around his ankle. He wrapped the length of rope into a coil. "Don't try to run off again, Audra. There are worse things than me out there that can hurt you." He motioned for her to lift her foot so he could free her ankle.

In a huff, Audra shot back. "What could be more dangerous than you?"

Tossing the rope aside, he squatted to stoke life into the campfire's dying embers. He poured water from his canteen into a coffeepot and added ground coffee. With his back to her, he said, "Mountain lion, coyotes, Apache, Comanche. Take your pick."

"Take me home, McKenna."

"Nope. Not just yet, Audra Tadlock. You're useful, and as long as you stay that way, I'll need you. When your use is finished, I'll take care of you."

Audra's long-lashed blue eyes widened. Take care of her? Why did he make it sound so ominous, so final?

He poured strong hot coffee into a cup. "Here, drink this while I fry up some bacon and beans."

He offered her a laconic smile. "Starting tonight, you'll do the cooking."

****

McKenna met Audra's wide stare and knew what she was thinking. So, let her think he'd kill her. It might keep her from any foolhardy acts. But somehow, he doubted it. The girl had proven she had spunk.

He set his cup aside. "Your last name always been Tadlock?"

She responded with a puzzled frown. "Of course. Is there a reason you should doubt me?"

"Sometimes people try to hide by changing their name."

Offering a defiant glare, she measured her words. "Being sisters, Aunt Sophie and my mother were Andersons. My father was John Tadlock. When the

Yankees killed my parents and burned our farm, Aunt Sophie scratched together all the money she could, and we fled to Texas. I was born a Tadlock, and I'll die a Tadlock."

Her heaving chest caused the tight shirt she wore to strain across her small yet perfectly rounded breasts, outlining them and leaving little to his imagination. Miss Audra Tadlock didn't know it, but it had taken all his self-control to stay on his own blankets during the night. He'd been too aware of her womanliness when he'd removed her clothing and dressed her in Billy Watt's britches and shirt that he'd stolen off the backyard clothesline before leaving town.

An unwilling smile crooked McKenna's mouth. He gazed at Audra through narrowed eyes. "You have a brother, maybe could be a twin brother, named Bubba Buchanan?"

Audra wiped her hands on her pants. She set the plate of beans aside and tried to meet his gaze. "Either you are deaf, or stupid, or both. I just finished explaining that—" Warily eyeing him, she hesitated as if not quite certain how to continue. "Did you say...twin brother?"

"So you're admitting Buchanan is your brother?"

"No, I'm not, but I did have a twin. Mama used to say we were like two peas in the same pod." Her voice softened to a whisper. "He died."

"When?"

"Long time ago. His name was Andrew Jackson Tadlock. We called him—Andy."

"Tell me about your brother, Audra. How did he die?"

"Andy loved to fish on the bayou. Papa was always

warning him not to go out in the boat." Tears glistened on her lashes. "Sometimes there were 'gators. Papa was afraid Andy might fall out of the boat and drown...or worse, get...eaten."

McKenna scooped a spoonful of beans into his mouth. He chewed thoughtfully for a moment. "He tetched in the head, this brother of yours?"

Audra said nothing but sat with her arms curved around her knees, keeping her thoughts to herself. When she looked up, she shrugged. "I dunno. He was different than the neighbor boys. Mama said it was because of his accident."

"Different in what way, Audra? It's important."

She rose abruptly from the ground and paced back and forth. McKenna watched the emotions playing on her face. He reached across the smoldering embers for the tin cup and refilled it with coffee. "Sit down, Audra."

Accepting the cup, she obeyed, then lifted her chin and gazed directly into his eyes. "I don't know why this is so important to you, or why you think this Bubba Buchanan is my brother. All I can tell you is that before he died, Andy was different. Mama said something unclicked in his brain during birthing. Then one day she put him down for a nap, and he rolled off the bed. A huge knot rose up on his forehead. If Andy was different from birth, he was even more different as he grew older." She stopped long enough to wet her throat with tepid coffee.

McKenna watched the girl across from him struggling to share what was probably a family secret. He waited, giving her time to collect her thoughts.

"My brother...my twin...was a sweet, beautiful

boy…sometimes. Most times, though, I'm ashamed to admit that he took pleasure in hurting things." Audra released an audible sigh. "Mama always blamed herself, and even though Andy died, I think there was a sense of relief in"—the last words were almost inaudible—"in all of us."

Audra swiped the tears collecting on her cheeks. "Papa spotted our boat floating in the grass flats. Even though he figured Andy might have drowned or was eaten by 'gators, we searched the shorelines, the swamps, the fields."

McKenna lifted enigmatic eyes to her face. "Did you ever find his body?"

Her voice grew suddenly shrill as it cut in on him. "If it weren't for the damned Blue-bellies—" She lowered her head to her knees and cried, her shoulders rising and falling with each sob.

He was the cause of her tortured memories. He'd obviously touched on something much deeper than the death of her twin. He went to sit beside her, and, reaching out with his left arm, he brought her slender body forward and kissed her. The violence of his own feelings made him hold her longer than he intended. It made the kiss rough and bruising. She pulled away, startled and angry. A pink stain covered her cheeks.

"Why did you do that, McKenna?"

"Because I had to—and wanted to."

"Do you always do what you want to do?"

"Most of the time," he admitted, showing her a smile. Then he added soberly, "What did you mean about the Blue-bellies?"

Audra shook her head. "No more, McKenna. Leave me alone, kill me, take me back to Hopeville. Do whatever it is you intend to do with me, but I don't want to talk about my brother or what happened after the Yankees came to our farm."

She rubbed her arms up and down the sleeves of her shirt. "I hear water. Is there a stream nearby?"

He untied the knot and slipped the rope from her ankle. Pointing the way, his eyes narrowed. "Wouldn't pay to run off."

After nearly tripping over a vine, she turned back to him, her eyes narrowed to slits. "Don't ever touch me again. If you do, I'll find a way to cut your heart out."

He watched her stumble through the brush. He hadn't realized how innocent she was until he'd kissed her, and it hit him like a kick in the head.

He suddenly recognized how clumsy her kiss had been, how untrained the slender arms were that had risen to wind around his neck. She had no idea how to return passion, and that had cooled his desire before she'd planted her hands against his chest and shoved him away.

He swore softly. He was a man who enjoyed challenges, and maybe being alone with Audra wasn't such a good idea after all. He listened to the words inside his head as if Ortiz were standing next to him. *Amigo, you are one muy loco hombre.*

McKenna removed the Colt .45 from his holster and spun the cylinder. He thumbed back the hammer, eased it back in place, sighted down the barrel, then snugged the revolver back inside the holster. *Maybe I should take her back to Hopeville.*

Long after she'd left him to go to the nearby stream, McKenna turned her words over in his mind and tried to read some shade of sense into them. It still didn't answer the question of whether Andy Tadlock and Bubba Buchanan were the same person.

****

Audra's senses reeled. She hadn't expected her fiery reaction to McKenna's kiss. Pressed close against him, she'd felt the hard thrust of his body against hers, the sinewy strength in his arms, and the erotic movement of his mouth over her lips. He'd held her so close she felt like she was drowning in a pool of warm liquid.

Was she as depraved as he was? Where had all her girlhood teachings gone—the ones about how a woman was to save her womanly virtues for the wedding bed? She pressed her hands to her hot cheeks.

To cool the molten blood flowing through her veins, she rose abruptly from the rock, and, fully dressed, splashed into the stream's cold water.

Chapter Five

Choking on the dust stirred up by the wind and McKenna's horse, Audra urged the donkey to a faster pace. "McKenna," she yelled, "doesn't this animal have more than one speed?"

McKenna grinned over his shoulder. "Flick him with the whip. Gotta show him you're boss."

She happened to drive the cart too close to the gelding and the cantankerous animal laid back its ears and nipped at the donkey, sending the slow-plodding animal skittering sideways and tipping the cart at a dangerous angle.

"How much farther to the outlaws' hideout?" She flashed McKenna a murderous glance.

"It's a ways yet. Waco is about twenty miles. We'll spend a few days there."

"A town? Are we sleeping in a hotel with beds, and maybe they'll have a bathtub?" Audra flicked the tip of the whip between the donkey's ears. After ten days of traveling and sleeping on the hard ground, she didn't think she'd ever been so hot and dirty in all her life. And McKenna had taken her threat to heart. He'd not tried to kiss her again, and he'd slept on his side of the campfire. She forced back a smile as a kernel of an idea began to sprout.

****

The day was nearly gone by the time McKenna

pointed to where they would stop for the night. "You set up camp, Audra. Think I'll see if I can bag us a couple of prairie hens for supper. I seem to recall that you make a good pot of chicken and dumplings."

She watched him ride away. Excitement filled her as she reined in the donkey. Not wasting time unhitching the gentle, doe-eyed animal from the cart, she climbed over the seat to where McKenna's camera and photography supplies lay stored inside a canvas-covered crate.

In the waning light, she spotted the saddlebags. With deft fingers, she unbuckled the straps and searched inside until her fingers touched the cold hard barrel. *I knew it. I knew he'd have a gun hidden away.* Wrapping her hands around the weapon, she withdrew a derringer. A quick check showed the small pistol held two shots.

Again she reached into the saddlebags and felt inside, searching for more bullets. When she didn't find any, she vowed to make the two she had hit their mark.

Slipping the weapon inside her pants pocket, she unhitched the donkey and hobbled him for the night. She gathered twigs and small branches to bank a fire, then set water to boil for the chicken, if McKenna got one.

She laid out her bedroll for the night. Biting down on her lip, she was determined that if she had to put a bullet through his heart, tonight she would escape and make her way to Waco, where she would purchase a stagecoach ticket back home and to the safety of Aunt Sophie. Automatically, she felt her pockets. *Money! I have no money.* Determined not to let a small thing like being penniless deter her from her plan, she decided to cross that bridge when she came to it.

She sat nursing a cup of coffee when McKenna returned holding a prairie hen like it was a prized trophy. Rehearsing every detail of her escape in her head, she silently plucked the bird.

"You're mighty quiet tonight, Audra. Got something on your mind?"

Damn. For days, I've rattled on non-stop about this and that and everything. Naturally he'd think I'm up to something. She hoped he couldn't read her mind.

She shrugged her shoulders as she dropped cut-up pieces of fowl into the pot and spooned dumplings into boiling water. "Nothing. Just wishing I had some seasoning and milk. I'm afraid plain flour and water doesn't make for tasty dumplings."

Think, you ninny. Think of something to say. He'll get suspicious...ooh!

"How did you learn to take pictures, McKenna?"

He was silent for a moment. "My father taught me. He had his own shop."

She didn't know why she was surprised at this declaration. Somehow she'd never thought of McKenna as having a family.

"You're not from Texas, are you?"

"Now, why would you think that, little girl?"

"Because sometimes there is a refinement to the way you speak—as if you are more educated than the average...what are you, a photographer, a cowboy, or an outlaw?"

McKenna slanted a sideways glance. "Well, I'm not a cowboy, that's for damn sure."

She picked up a pebble and tossed it at him. "Stop making fun of me. I don't like being treated as if I'm stupid."

"All right. My mother was a teacher. We lived in York, Pennsylvania. The Rebs came, burned most of the town, along with our home. My mother had a bad heart. Thankfully she died before seeing my father gunned down because he refused to take photographs for the Confederacy. And before you ask, I was sixteen. And did I join the Union? Yeah."

"It must have hurt you deeply to witness your parents' tragedy." Memories of her own parents' cruel deaths assailed her.

Audra's heart lurched when he strode to the cart, then settled again when he flung back the canvas and opened the burlap sack that held several bottles of whiskey. Instinctively, her hand felt for the derringer hidden deep inside her pants pocket.

They supped in silence. McKenna drank more than he ate. Bleary-eyed, he waved the bottle toward her. "You got any soul-baring secrets, little girl?" Before she answered, he said, "Nah, you've led a sheltered life."

She gave a mock sigh. "I don't have any skeletons in my closets, McKenna. Not like you."

He tipped the bottle to his lips and swigged deep, then drew the sleeve of his shirt across his mouth. His words were slurred, his eyes bleary. "Wadda you mean—skeletons?"

"You're no ordinary photographer, McKenna. I may be young and naïve, but I don't think wearing a tied-down six-gun is a prerequisite for taking pictures."

He tipped the bottle again and, finding it empty, tossed it aside. He squinted at her. "You don't know nothing, Aud—" Before he could finish her name, he lay back and filled the night with thunderous snores.

Audra gathered the pot of leftovers and walked a short distance from the camp. She scraped the pot's remains onto the ground.

Hurrying back toward the fire, she wondered why he hadn't tried to kiss her again. *Maybe he thinks I'll make good on my threat.* This surprised her. She'd seen him staring at her several times, his eyes lingering on the way the tight shirt strained across her breasts. But he'd done nothing.

Perversely, this irritated Audra. Perhaps it was because she looked terrible with her chopped-off hair, clothes that made her look like a boy, and no soap to wash away grime and body odor. She could hardly be blamed for looking her worst, could she?

The gelding's nervous whinnies drew away her thoughts. The animal reared against his hobbles. She walked to the horse, ran her hands down his neck, and spoke soothing words. "What's got you spooked, huh?"

The gelding tossed its head up and down and nickered when a coyote yipped somewhere in the distance and was answered by another. The little donkey brayed. The undulating echoes of coyote howls rippled through the night.

Audra's resolve to escape melted away with fear— fear of leaving and fear of staying. She berated herself for dumping the food scraps so close to camp. In her haste to make her escape, she'd forgotten McKenna's warning to never dump food scraps near the camp. Generally, there wasn't enough food left over each night to worry about.

She waited in tense silence, listening to sniffing and the padding of feet nearby. She eased back to the fire, tossed on another branch, and watched sparks flare. Gathering her blanket, she tucked herself next to McKenna. She decided to sleep a bit, then saddle the horse and head for Waco before the break of dawn.

****

After a restless night, Audra awoke at the peak of dawn. She eased up on her knees, pushed to her feet and took several eager steps forward, then paused uncertainly. She was suddenly afraid, yet knew it might be her only chance. She could get away on the horse, but she needed money. If she went to the sheriff in Waco, would he believe her story? Could Aunt Sophie afford to wire stage fare? Would McKenna come after her? And worse, what if he did?

There were many things that could happen—maybe now wasn't the right time to try an escape. Deciding a botched attempt would only make matters worse, she wearily turned and with a slow step headed back to her blanket.

It was the slightest movement that caused the nerve in her jaw to tense. She blinked to clear her vision. Fear coiled in her belly as lethal as the rattler slithering toward McKenna. She inched her hand inside her pocket and withdrew the derringer. Trembling hands made it difficult to thumb back the hammer.

In a low, petrified voice, she hissed, "McKenna, don't move. Dear God, don't move. *McKenna*—"

She fearfully wondered if she could make at least one shot count.

****

Fringes of light played with the morning casting a ray over McKenna's face. His mouth was dry, and he wondered when his tongue had grown fur. The last thing he wanted to hear was Audra's voice cutting into his sleep or to have sunlight blind him. He grunted, coughed, and squinted up at her through one eye.

The derringer pointed at him caused him to open the other eye. "What the hell—"

"Shut up and don't move." Audra's voice pitched higher. Her expression was grim as she gazed beyond his shoulder.

He rose up on one elbow, a smirk on his face. "Guess the hair-of-the-dog bit me good last night."

"Something else is going to bite you if you don't shut up and stay still." She spoke through clenched teeth. "S-snake."

"Not very original, Audra. Put the gun down before you hurt yourself—or worse, me." The moment he shifted, cold ripples of tension prickled his scalp. The ominous whirring stilled him.

His mouth a thin, tight line, he said, "Pull the trigger."

Beads of perspiration formed on his furrowed brow, and he found himself at the mercy of a girl who looked as if she might faint any minute. His body began to ache at the awkward position of supporting himself on one elbow. A rock gouged into his hip, adding to his discomfort.

"Damn it all to hell, girl! Pull the damn trigger."

Her breath coming in short, quick gasps, she pressed her lips together. Her finger tightened around the trigger. "What if I miss?"

Trembling, she used both hands to keep from dropping the derringer.

The panic on her face worried him. Which worse, a slow death from the bite of a venomous snake, or gangrene from a bullet wound? *Hell of a choice.*

"Pull the trigger, girl. Do it!"

Audra sucked in a breath and held it. She closed one eye and squinted down the barrel with the other as she extended her arms. In her nervousness, she fired twice in rapid succession.

Muzzle flame sent red ribbons pulsing through the morning light. McKenna felt a hot breath of air as the first bullet whizzed past him. A torn cry of anguish caused him to reel sideways as the second slug tore through the flesh of his right arm.

"Hellfire! You shot me!" He looked incredulous.

"And you cut off my hair. At least the snake is dead. Be thankful for small miracles. I could have killed you."

Gripping his bloodied arm, he leapt from the spot. She'd blown the rattler's head clean off. He had no doubt he was one lucky hombre.

Chapter Six

Audra watched the blood, like a crimson curtain, staining McKenna's shirt. Appalled at wounding him, she dashed to his side. "I've never fired a gun before."

"Hell, Audra, reckon you've saved me from a painful death. Dying from a rattler's bite takes hours, sometimes days."

Revulsion shuddered through her as she reached out with frantic hands, grasping his arm. "Don't stand there bleeding all over the place. I may not know how to shoot, but I do know a little about doctoring."

When his eyebrows winged up in surprised bemusement, she said, "When business is slow at the dress shop, I sometimes help Doctor Atwater."

She knelt behind McKenna, sliding the shirt from his shoulders. In spite of the heat, she shivered. "Who did this to you?" Her voice rasped as she reached out and touched the puckered skin covering three symmetrical scars that marred his broad back.

"Doesn't matter. Your petticoats...hell, you found the derringer. You already know where they are."

When she rose to sprint to the cart, he yelled, "Bring a bottle of whiskey."

Whirling around, she raked him with a scathing glance. He responded with a handsomely wicked grin. "Strictly medicinal."

Kneeling over the fire, Audra placed the skinning

knife on a rock to heat the blade. She took little pleasure when McKenna winced against the pain as she poured whiskey over the torn flesh.

"Thank goodness it's only a flesh wound."

He answered with a grunt.

She drew the knife from the fire but hesitated before laying the hot blade against his flesh to cauterize the wound. "This is going to hurt." She handed him the bottle. "Here."

He lifted it to his lips and chugged deeply. He sucked in a deep breath and nodded.

Every nerve raw and tense, she fought down the roiling nausea threatening to spill from her throat at the odor of searing flesh. She watched McKenna's jaw work under the pain, watched him blink to clear his vision. From the healed scars where bullets had exited through his chest, she knew he'd survived worse.

She tore the hem of her petticoat into strips and bandaged his arm. "It was Bubba Buchanan who shot you, wasn't it?"

He nodded.

"That's why you kidnapped me. You're using me as bait because you think he's my brother?"

"Smart girl."

"He shot you in the back. Why?" She watched the tenseness in his face and, when he didn't answer, said, "If you're going to kill him, and then me, too, the least you can do is offer me an explanation."

"Fair enough. If you'll tell me about the Blue-bellies, as you so aptly called the Union soldiers." His voice was quiet, surprisingly gentle.

She mentally told herself he was cruel. He was rough. But the fact remained that he'd struck a chord in her heart. She was surprised and had the sudden urge to reach out and touch him. This man had known loneliness and hardship.

****

McKenna's eyes searched Audra's. He was curious and suddenly aware there was more to this woman than strange blue eyes and hair the color of cornsilk. He didn't think she was aware of her own beauty. He looked down at the cup of coffee she had poured him and had a sudden hope that she wouldn't witness him kill Bubba Buchanan. Whatever happened, he wanted to protect her from that. For a long moment, their eyes held, searching, measuring. He wanted to reach out and touch the quivering smile that played on her lips.

"I met up with Pete Buchanan a few days after he'd found the boy. Kid had a high fever and was ranting out of his mind. Apparently he'd gone fishing and, it being a hot day, decided to go swimming. When he dove into the water, a current caught him and swept him away from the boat. When Buchanan found the boy, he'd been bitten by a water moccasin.

"Buchanan normally doesn't have a charitable bone in his body. Don't know why, but he nursed this boy back to health, told people the kid was his adopted son. When the boy couldn't remember his name, fellows in the gang started calling him Bubba."

Audra listened wide-eyed to McKenna. "In the South, anyone called *Bubba* generally isn't quite right in the head."

"Exactly." McKenna cradled his aching arm. "From the outset, it was obvious the boy had a natural mean streak. Buchanan taught the kid how to shoot, took him on raids. After the war, and with no homes or families waiting for us, we robbed banks, trains, stage coaches, freight lines—" McKenna reached for the bottle and laced his coffee with whiskey. After a sip, he tossed out the bitter brew.

"Bubba turned into a killing machine. Men, women—the last straw, for me, was a little girl after a bank job that'd gone bad. She reminded me of a broken doll, all crumpled into a heap. He liked killing so much that afterward he'd bray like a damned jackass in heat.

"Even with the posse hot on our tails, I couldn't get the image of that little girl out of my head. I'd planned to collect my share of the take and cut ties with the gang—made the mistake of telling Pete why I was leaving. Made a bigger mistake when I turned my back on Bubba.

"The posse found me more dead than alive. I spent five years in a federal pen." He stopped short of telling her he'd been pardoned by the governor on the condition that he bring in Pete Buchanan and his gang—dead or alive.

****

Audra hung onto every word of McKenna's explanation, especially the part about Bubba Buchanan. She was drenched. She had broken out into a cold sweat. She wanted to laugh, to cry, to reach out and slap McKenna's handsome face. Bubba Buchanan wasn't her brother. Knowing she had to ask the question, she felt brittle.

"When you joined up with Buchanan, did he say where he'd found the boy?" She asked the question— afraid of the answer.

"I'd been separated from my unit before making my way to Charleston. That's where I met up with

Sergeant Buchanan and his raiders. Said he'd found the boy in the swamps about twenty miles east of town."

Standing abruptly, she practically shouted, desperation ringing in her voice. "None of this proves anything. Bubba Buchanan isn't Andy. Do you hear me, McKenna?"

McKenna was right behind her. He wrapped his arms around her trembling body. "I hope to God you're right."

She twisted in his arms and beat her fists against his chest. When she landed a blow to his wounded arm, he muttered an oath and abruptly released her.

Blinded by tears, she raced to the horse and yanked hard to untie the slipknot that secured the lead rope to the tree. Grabbing a fistful of mane, Audra swung Indian-style onto the gelding's bare back. She kicked the horse in the flanks, urging him into a run—forgetting the animal was still hobbled from the night before.

The gelding reared, sending Audra tumbling from his bare back. She lay on the ground and succumbed to tears till there were none left—only the empty, aching pain of her lost childhood and uncertain future.

Chapter Seven

The week passed with agonizing slowness until Audra guided the donkey cart down the dusty streets of Waco. Except for passing an occasional word, she'd closed off her emotions and stayed to herself.

With application of fresh bandages every few days, the flesh wound on McKenna's arm continued to heal without fear of infection.

She glanced around. Little more than wind-peeled buildings and a crudely painted sign identified the town. It was late afternoon, and the sun had begun to sink in a fiery red ball behind a distant horizon. Still the street was a beehive of activity. A crowd gathered in a clump.

"McKenna, what's happening?" Audra pulled the donkey to a halt.

"Don't know. Pull over, and stay put." He swung out of the saddle and tied the horse to the rear of the cart.

Tension crackled between them as they glared at each other. McKenna turned and sprinted toward the group of people. He pushed forward. Three men lay dead. "What happened here?"

A man wearing an apron spoke. "This here feller and a bunch of others tried to rob the bank. Poor ole Tompkins and Evers were minding their own business—gunned down like dogs, they were."

"You know who did it?" McKenna's left arm ached its usual warning.

"Sure do. Tow-headed kid with eyes the color of death. And he laughed—laughed like it was some kinda joke." The man lifted the corner of his apron and dabbed at his eyes. "Weren't no sense in it, neither. Ole Tompkins never hurt a fly, and Evers, well, he was half blind."

The sheriff and a posse rode up. "Care to join us, Mister?"

McKenna said, "I'm a photographer, Sheriff. My business is taking pictures of outlaws, not hunting 'em down."

"Pictures, huh? You know that piece of buzzard bait?"

McKenna reached up and scratched his jaw. "Yep. Roy Halstead. One of Pete Buchanan's men."

"Hellfire." The sheriff swore as he spurred his horse into action. "Let's get a move on, men. We're burning daylight."

McKenna left the crowd and sprinted to where Audra patiently waited. "Stay out of sight until I get back."

"Why? What's happened?"

"Damn, girl. Do you always have to question everything I ask?" McKenna reached out and gripped Audra's chin, his calloused fingers digging into her soft skin. "There's three dead men over there. One rode with Buchanan. The others were innocent bystanders." McKenna turned and pointed. "See that old man wearing the apron?" He didn't wait for Audra's response. "He described the killer. And the killer looks just like you. What'll you think will happen if that old man spots you?"

Audra's throat was suddenly dry. Her heart pounded furiously. "Okay, I'll stay put. But where are you going?"

"To get you a hat." He looked her up and down. "And a bigger shirt."

****

Audra jammed the slouch hat down on her head. She struggled to keep the saddlebags from sliding off her shoulder while wrestling with the tripod. McKenna toted the camera and a box of pewter plates. Keeping her eyes downcast, she followed him across the street.

The crowd had subsided, and the undertaker and his assistant were lifting the dead bodies into coffins. McKenna approached the undertaker. "I'd like to photograph that one." He pointed to the outlaw.

The undertaker nodded. "Better make it quick, mister. In this heat, won't take long for 'em to start stinkin'."

McKenna nodded. "Boy, after you set up the tripod, go on over to the hotel and get us a room." He reached into his pocket and flipped Audra a five-dollar gold piece. "And go to the kitchen and order up some dinner. We'll eat in our room tonight."

His face might have been hewn from mahogany when she looked at him. Wasting no time after she spread the tripod's legs apart, she sidestepped away from the coffins and hot-footed it toward the hotel.

****

Audra ordered two steak dinners with whipped potatoes and gravy, biscuits, and a pot of coffee. She also ordered a tub and buckets of hot water.

When she walked from the kitchen balancing a tray

of food in one hand and a coffeepot in the other, the clerk said, "Sent the tub and water up."

In her deepest voice, she thanked him. Once inside the room, she set the tray on top of the dresser and lifted her plate of food, placing a towel over McKenna's to keep it warm.

The steak was tough, the gravy lumpy, and the potatoes too salty. Her trail food tasted better than this. She pushed the less-than-delectable meal aside.

Shedding the clothes she'd worn for most of a month, she kicked them aside and stepped into the tub of hot water. She wrinkled her nose as she sniffed the bar of lye soap. It wasn't like her lilac-scented soap back home. An overwhelming feeling of despair settled over her. Home and Aunt Sophie—Audra missed them both.

She scrubbed the layers of grime on her skin, lathered her hair and massaged her scalp, then submerged herself under the water. She came up sputtering and pushing back wet hair. And then, she lay back and luxuriated in the tub until the water grew cold.

When she was certain she heard no booted steps approaching the room, she climbed out of the tub and wrapped herself in a towel. She then set about washing her only set of clothes, wringing out most of the water and setting them over two straight-back chairs to dry.

Opening one of the saddle bags, she pulled out her undergarments and put them on. The petticoat was much shorter since using part of the skirt as bandages for McKenna's arm.

Sliding down on the bed with a contented sigh, Audra lay back and closed her eyes. It felt good to sleep on a mattress after weeks of lying on hard ground.

She let her mind drift, thinking of Andy. She tried to visualize his boyish face, the quirky grin, the sound of his laughter. McKenna's earlier words crept inside her thoughts—*and the killer looks just like you.*

She rolled to her side, burying her face in the pillow. She tried to drag her thoughts away from her brother and concentrate on how frantic Aunt Sophie must be. Perhaps McKenna would allow her to send a telegram letting her aunt know that she was alive.

Unfortunately, thoughts of McKenna kept popping into Audra's head. She visualized him at their first encounter, when she'd nearly toppled his camera from its stand, how he'd sent her scurrying across the floor of the dress shop to keep her from getting shot, and the way he'd kissed her when she'd become upset after he'd told how the Confederate soldiers had killed his parents.

Who was McKenna Smith? She decided he was an educated man who'd descended to the ranks of a common outlaw, just like the men he was following. By planning to use her as bait to lure out Bubba, he was no better than any member of Buchanan's gang.

Her mouth tightened in irritation. She sighed. *What a situation to be in.*

****

The hotel room was hotter than the August night. McKenna stood until his eyes adjusted to the darkness. Moonlight filtered through a slit in the curtain, outlining Audra's lithe form. She lay on her side, her hands folded under her chin. The shortened petticoat had ridden up, exposing the creamy flesh of her hip.

He wanted so badly to feel the softness of her skin, to ease his fingers through the richness of her silken tresses. He wanted to feel the whispery softness of her breath upon his cheek, her mouth pressed gently to his own. He imagined her in the arms of another man and jealousy raged within him.

Deeply lost in his thoughts, he scarcely realized he had tiptoed to the window and opened it, until a stingy breath of air filtered into the room.

He'd deliberately stayed away, giving her the privacy she needed to enjoy a long and uninterrupted bath. Even he had sought comfort in a public bathhouse, washing away miles of perspiration and dirt. While soaking in a tub of hot sudsy water, he'd enjoyed a strong cigar and a glass of smooth rye whiskey. And he'd thought about Audra. What was he going to do with her once he killed Bubba Buchanan? Once she realized the outlaw was her brother, McKenna knew she'd hate him. There was no turning back. His decision was made. He felt a moment of anguish that quickened the pace of his heart.

He sat on the chair and removed his boots. Unbuckling his gun belt and laying it aside, he shed his freshly washed and ironed clothes.

The moonlight played across the porcelain-skinned beauty. McKenna's body tightened into an iron-hard betrayer. An ache crawled down to his belly, entering his groin so quickly he felt almost compelled to dive into the tub of cold water left behind from Audra's earlier bath.

In one fluid move, he eased onto the bed, molding his body around hers. He had no doubt she was a virgin. Though guilt flooded through him, his body was like an explosion that refused to be denied the sweetness of her treasure.

His fingers moved up the scant material of her petticoat, halting as she opened her eyes. He saw the dazed confusion, and then the fear. His voice was a raspy whisper. "Don't be frightened, Audra. I'll try not to hurt you."

When she shyly attempted to cover herself, he took her hands and held them to his chest. "We both knew this moment would happen. It was only a matter of when." He lowered his mouth to hers.

****

McKenna's hips straddled her, and Audra felt the hardness of him against her abdomen. When he released his kiss, his mouth descended to capture the rosy peak of one breast. Audra drew in a quick breath of air. What was McKenna doing to her? What was he doing to make her want more than she could imagine in her wildest dreams? Without her willing it, her body surged upward. Panic and wondrous anticipation seized her from within and shook her to reality. She placed her hands against his chest. "No…stop. I beg you to stop."

With a low growl, he drew her to his body. His left hand lowered, and his fingers found the treasure he was seeking—moist, warm, and begging for his attention.

Audra's body stiffened. "This is wrong… Don't you understand? I can't… Please, McKenna, it's indecent."

Her pleas dampened his desire, and he rolled away from her to grab his pants off the chair and cover himself. She curled into a ball and tried to mute her weeping. When the sobs stilled, she sat on the edge of the bed. McKenna wrapped a strong arm around her shoulder. She sat beside him, her hand tenderly enfolded within his own, her eyes downcast. She listened first to the deep sigh he expelled, then to his softly spoken words.

"Making love is a natural act between a man and a woman, Audra. It isn't wrong or indecent unless you make it that way."

She shuddered, every nerve raw and tense. Her thoughts drifted back to the nightmare, and in the darkness she once more saw her mother's face and heard how she begged the Yankee soldiers to stop. Would she ever be able to forget, or would she forever be haunted because she'd been too young to protect her mother?

"Audra?"

Chapter Eight

The unbearable heat was not relieved by the breeze wandering in through the open window, and a thin layer of perspiration became an adhesive between Audra's hand and McKenna's.

"Audra?" McKenna repeated her name. "Talk to me."

She fought for a moment of calm within the confines of his closeness and caught her breath as the sound of her name sifted into her ear. His musky scent assailed her delicate senses, and unthinkingly, she leaned her head to rest against his shoulder.

"The day the Yankees rode into the yard, Mama was hanging wash on the line, and Papa was inside the barn. I was in the kitchen helping Aunt Sophie prepare lunch.

"Mama's scream drew us to the window. She tried to rush to the house, but several of the soldiers jumped from their horses and grabbed her. Her screams brought Papa running from the barn. His only weapon was a pitchfork. He was shot down in cold blood."

Audra shuddered. "I remember seeing the ground turn red. Before I could cry out, Aunt Sophie clamped her hand over my mouth. She said we must be brave and not let the soldiers know we were in the house.

"She grabbed my hand, and we eased out the kitchen door and crawled underneath the house and tucked ourselves behind the back steps.

"I could see what those men were doing to Mama. She pleaded with them to stop. They kept taking turns, and she kept screaming, and when the screams stopped, the damned Blue-belly dogs didn't even bother to pull her skirt down. They laughed. And then we heard them inside the house, going from room to room, and swilling the food we'd fixed."

Audra frowned darkly, remembering the carefree days before the war. Now she was a confused shell of a woman, wanting to love the man next to her yet afraid to trust him. She felt the strength of his arms as he held her.

When he didn't speak, she knew he was giving her time to collect her emotions so she could continue.

"One of the soldiers found Papa's store of coal oil. After they'd filled their bellies and ransacked the house, they set fire to the house and barn. I thought we would die...burn to death hiding there behind the kitchen steps. And then they rode out—leaving Mama and Papa lying in the dirt. As soon as we were certain the soldiers were gone, we crawled from beneath the house. The floors were already on fire and the smoke was scorching our lungs.

"Ole Mose, he's a freed man who did odd jobs for Papa, saw the smoke and came to investigate. He helped us bury my parents."

Suddenly, tears rushed upon her, but she lowered her gaze and discreetly brushed away the evidence of her sorrow. Feeling perfectly miserable, she rose from the bed, caring not a whit that the shortened hem of her petticoat exposed her slender legs.

McKenna stirred from the bed, and his hands

gripped her shoulders, drawing her back to him. "Let me chase away your hurts, Audra. I can think of nothing more challenging than making you happy…to be with me."

She wanted to enjoy his nearness, to hear the soft laughter in his voice. She wished the tender moments could go on forever. On the other hand, she wondered how long it would be before he said something to completely destroy the mood.

"How can I be happy with you, McKenna, when you've vowed to kill the man you claim is my twin brother?"

His arms dropped away from her. With furious jerks, he tugged on his shirt, jamming the shirttail into the waistband of his pants. He strapped on his gun belt and grabbed his hat. Giving her a somewhat beleaguered look, he stepped past her and yanked the door open.

When Audra gently touched his arm, he shrugged it off. "Be ready to move out at dawn. We have a rendezvous with the devil."

****

Accustomed to sleeping in short snatches, when and where it was possible, McKenna's body could not attune itself to long, unrestricted rest. Despite his weariness, he awakened suddenly and with a start. "Damn woman."

Groggily, he sat up and ran his fingers through his hair. His body felt heavy and his mouth tasted bad. He stood and brushed straw from his clothes. He strode outside to the horse trough and dunked his head, filled his mouth with water, then spat it onto the ground.

He called out to the hostler, "Have the horses

saddled. Soon as I collect a package from the hotel, I'll be ready to ride."

The hostler said, "Sure 'nuf, hoss. When you comin' back to get your equipment?"

"Soon as my business is done with a former associate."

McKenna walked up the street toward the hotel, his boots grating on the hard-packed dirt. It was nearly dawn, but there were still stars. A few stores showed the dull glow of a lamp, and he heard the murmur of voices. The moment he stepped up on the boardwalk in front of the hotel, he was hit by a force that rocked him back on his heels.

"'Scuse me, Mister. I'm in a hurry."

McKenna sliced Audra a hard look. "When you didn't show up at the livery, I thought you might've run out on me."

"And where would I go without any money?" Audra met his gaze without flinching.

In that instant, McKenna changed his mind. He grabbed her wrist. "I'm putting you on a stage back to your aunt."

"No." Audra vehemently shook her head.

"Dammit, there's no sense arguing about this. If I have to drag you down the middle of the street to the stage office, you're going back to Hopeville, and back to your aunt. It's all I've heard from you for weeks."

She struggled against his tight grip as he moved away from the hotel doorway. "I'll get off the stage. I'll follow you."

She jerked her arm in a feeble attempt to loosen his painful hold.

"I can make it damned unpleasant for you on the

trail. We'll ride hard and fast, taking little time for rest or meals. If you know what's best, you'll go home, Audra."

"Don't you understand? I've got to prove to myself that Bubba Buchanan isn't my brother. I won't have any peace until I know." Her jaw settled into a solid, stubborn wedge. "Do your worst, McKenna. There's not a whole lot more you can do to humiliate or hurt me. You should know by now I'm not a person who is easily conquered."

McKenna gave a grudging nod of agreement. Never had he seen such immutable determination in a woman's face. He wanted to smile, but he ground his lips together. "No special considerations. When I say froggy, you jump." Then, pivoting on his boot heel, he headed toward the livery stable.

****

McKenna rode at a hard clip. Audra followed, closing the gap, riding the roan gelding he'd purchased back in Waco. She'd made several unsuccessful attempts to speak to McKenna when they paused at regular intervals to eat a cold meal of jerky washed down with water, and to rest the horses.

At the end of the third day, she urged her laboring mount to the top of a ridge. McKenna raised his hand, signaling her to stop.

He pointed. "Down there is Buchanan's stronghold. Can you keep up?"

Audra nodded. She followed McKenna, letting her horse twist its way down the brush-studded slope. As they moved in deeper darkness, she felt as if the night's silence surged forward to meet them, teeming with a sense of evil that was almost tangible.

138

They pushed on slowly, McKenna's gun hand primed and ready for action. The clip-clop of the ponies' hoofs echoed sharply in the stillness.

"Haul up, friends," a voice sang out from the shadows. "One wrong move and we'll blast you right outta your saddles."

"Fargo Wilson, that you?" McKenna responded in a gruff voice.

"Who's that?" snapped the outlaw hidden in the dark.

"McKenna Smith."

"Don't say. And who's the other gent?"

"Kid I picked up a while back." McKenna hesitated, searching for a name.

Audra felt herself turn faint and sick, but forced herself to sit still in the saddle. Pale and frightened, nevertheless she kept her voice strong as she spoke. "Andy Tadlock's the name, and killin's my game."

McKenna hissed under his breath, "Shut up, kid. You talk too much."

There was a split-second pause. The lookout lifted his voice. "McKenna. By God, you're one jasper I never thought to see again."

"Yeah, why's that?"

"Hell, the way that loco kid of Buchanan's filled you full of lead, figured you for a goner."

McKenna dropped his right hand to his gunstock. "Speaking of Buchanan, he in camp?"

"Nope. What's your business with Pete?"

"Got a score to settle with the boy."

"Don't blame you. Kid's like a rabid wolf—kills for no reason." The outlaw touched the sling that supported his right arm. "Kid clipped off a piece of my hide, busted my wing. He's gettin' outta control."

McKenna exchanged a brief glance with Audra. "Why doesn't Buchanan do something about it?"

The guard looked around as if the night had prying ears. "Just between you and me, I think Pete's afraid of the kid."

Audra remained in her slouching, indolent position. Inside, her nerves were raw. In the moonlight she saw the grim lines of McKenna's tightened lips.

"You're one lucky bastard, Fargo. Now, where did you say Pete was?"

"I know you're fast with a gun, McKenna. But you were a leftie. I doubt you're good enough with your right hand—that is if you're plannin' on callin' the kid out." A wicked grin flattened the outlaw's lips. "What the hell. Pete and the boys lit out no more'n an hour ago. Gone to Dry Wells to pull a job."

McKenna nodded at the outlaw. "No honor among thieves, eh, Fargo?"

As McKenna and Audra backed their horses down the draw, Fargo sang out, "See you in hell, McKenna."

****

As the moonlit night lengthened, it cast distorted patterns across the trail's hard surface. Foam flecked the weary horse beneath Audra. Her own perspiration dripped down her sides. Hot and sticky, her body ached from days of hard riding.

Ahead, McKenna seemed unaffected. He sat easily astride his sweating horse. Audra wondered how he could remain disturbingly cool.

Bone weary, she was tired of riding behind him, tired of watching his back for hours. Her feet and legs were numb, her arms and shoulders ached, and from the constant motion of her butt against the saddle, she was certain she'd need to grow a new hide. "My horse is going to fall out from under me if we don't stop soon. How much farther to Dry Wells?"

McKenna turned in his saddle to look at her and lifted an inquiring brow. "About five miles."

A chill skipped down her spine at the thought of what would happen once they caught up with Bubba Buchanan. She recalled the words of the outlaw, Fargo Wilson. *Kid's like a rabid wolf—kills for no good reason.*

If Bubba was truly her brother, would he recognize her? Would he be shocked she'd found him after all these years? She feared the disastrous results if he and McKenna fought each other.

When McKenna hadn't pushed his attentions on her, when he'd comforted her and listened to how the soldiers had abused her mother, when he'd opened his heart and offered to make her happy, it erased any doubts she'd had about him. Though exhaustion now dragged her down, there was a poignant emotion for this hard man that she'd never dreamed she could feel.

She would accept him for better or worse.

Her heart had chosen what her mind had rejected.

It would tear her in two if she had to choose between McKenna and her twin.

Chapter Nine

As they approached the town of Dry Wells, Audra squinted against the blinding light cutting across her vision. She lifted one hand to shade her eyes and spotted the glittering metal rails that curved across the land. A railroad meant a thriving town—a town filled with wealth.

Using the cattle pens that lined one end of the town as a shield, she and McKenna walked their horses. They rode on past the small building serving as the railroad station.

"McKenna, can't we forget about this and leave? I'll go anywhere you want. Please." Her mouth was dry, and she tugged the brim of her floppy hat lower over her eyes.

He cut her a razor-sharp glance. His easy half-sardonic manner was gone. So was his flashing smile. In their place was a gray-edged look about his mouth and a bitter black sheen in his eyes.

His voice hardened. "I tried to send you home—remember?"

****

McKenna rubbed his stubbled jaw ruefully. Hell, his patience had to hold out. He had the oddest feeling he should take Audra and ride on out of town.

The main road was clogged with people. The sun shined down on the assemblage, and dust rose to form a choking haze.

"What's happening, McKenna? Why are all these people in the street?"

He smiled stiffly, his eyes holding a residue of anger. "Seems we've missed Buchanan—again."

A man wearing mutton-chop sideburns and a sweeping mustache and hobbling on crutches pushed through the throng of people. He issued a speculative look toward McKenna and Audra. He brushed irritably at a fly that kept trying to land on his nose.

Noting the tin star on the man's vest, McKenna said, "What's all the ruckus, Sheriff?"

"Buchanan gang. They robbed the train just outside of Dry Wells early this morning. It held the payroll for the mines."

"You seem mighty certain it was Buchanan."

"Don't know that it's any of your business, Mister, but the kid with hair that matches the albino horse he rides was part of the gang. It was Buchanan, all right."

Audra kept her voice low and husky. "Did you catch any of 'em?"

The sheriff eyed her. "You look familiar, boy. I know you?" He inched closer for a better look.

McKenna cut his horse in between the sheriff and Audra's mount. "Never mind the kid. He talks too much. So I'll ask—you catch any of them?"

The gray-haired sheriff slanted McKenna a curious glance. "Slicker'n oil they are. Ain't worried, though— Federal marshals and my posse's after 'em. With any luck, they'll ride in soon."

"Know which way the gang headed, Sheriff?" McKenna shrugged matter-of-factly.

At that moment, the posse rode into town and

spectators surged forward to watch and listen.

McKenna tipped his hat. "'Scuse us, Sheriff."

****

Audra followed McKenna, scanning the faces of the handcuffed outlaws. All her concentration was focused on finding Andy. She didn't care about anything except getting to her brother before McKenna did.

She reined in her horse and stared at the three outlaws' grimy, sweat-covered faces. Relief surged through her, and then she spotted the body slung over the saddle. His head bobbled in rhythm with the horse's gait. Her breath hitched as she looked at the dead man—it wasn't Andy.

"Follow me to the livery, Audra. We'll trade our mounts for fresh horses. Then we'll have us a fine meal and sleep in a soft bed. The hotel has a bathtub. I'll order up some hot water for you."

Audra stared into the abyss of McKenna's dark eyes, moved by his gentle voice and his apparent attempt at kindness, yet she was still wary.

"Why aren't we following them now?"

"Because you are as done in as the horse you're riding. And so am I."

Outside the livery stable, her knees buckled when she swung out of the saddle. Her thoughts were broken and scattered. Exhaustion burned in her chest. Leading the gelding forward, she stumbled against McKenna's broad shoulder.

He reached out to cradle her elbow. His fingers brushed absently at the smudge on her cheek. "If it wouldn't draw attention to us, I'd sweep you off your feet and carry you to the hotel."

Audra dreaded the night ahead. She dreaded the morrow, when they would catch up with Buchanan's gang. And she dreaded the demons fighting within her. Moisture gathered on her lower lashes.

****

Lightning stabbed the night with iridescent forks. Standing on the hotel room's veranda, Audra prayed it would start pouring any time. Perhaps the rain would wash away Buchanan's tracks.

A fiery streak of white split the sky, and the wind blew her hair wildly across her face as she stepped back into the room and closed the doors. A last gust of wind blew out the oil lamp's flame, leaving the room unexpectedly dark. Audra struck her foot on the chair leg and tripped against the bed.

Reflecting on the day's activities, she gazed up at the ceiling. McKenna had ordered up a bath, and he'd had dinner for one sent up. After days of beef jerky and tepid water, she'd cleaned her plate, right down to the last green pea.

He'd left her alone to bathe in privacy, and he'd left her to dine alone.

Damn you, McKenna. I won't be your conquest. Rolling to her side, she pounded the pillow with her fist. She wanted to feel the alien desires flood her body, the awakening of hidden pleasures.

The hotel was quiet. An owl's shivering cry marked the night, and a coyote yipped somewhere in the distance. Long, dark minutes went on and on. Where was McKenna? She didn't know whether to be relieved or angry.

She rose from the bed and tiptoed to the door, pressed her ear against it, listened, and heard nothing.

****

Cigar smoke hung like a heavy cloud inside the Spotted Horse Saloon. McKenna looked at the fan of cards in his hand, then lifted his gaze to study the three players. Undecided about his next move, he made no raise, simply discarded a five of hearts and a seven of spades.

His mind was no longer on playing cards. He slapped the pasteboards on the table. "Fold, gents." He slugged down the last of his beer and pushed back his chair.

The card playing was over for the night, but he'd learned what he needed to know. Pete Buchanan had taken a slug in the leg during the train robbery.

McKenna decided to bed down in an empty horse stall and ride out before dawn. He'd let Audra cool her heels at the hotel until he returned, and then he'd buy her a one-way ticket back to her aunt.

Stepping from the saloon, he inhaled the air sweetened by the rain. Mud sucked at his boots as he made his way to the livery stable.

Snuggled down in the straw, his saddle for a pillow, the memories of Audra's supple breast and soft lips sang in McKenna's entire body. He thought of the way her short hair framed her finely sculptured face, of the strange, almost colorless blue eyes that looked at him so provocatively, of smooth, warm skin the shade of ivory. No not quite that pale, more sun-kissed now. He rolled to his side as new and confusing thoughts arose.

Audra was right about one thing. He had behaved dishonorably, at least in terms of forcing his attentions on her.

As much as she excited and intrigued him, he decided to make his goodbyes by way of a note and leave enough money she could buy her own damned ticket back to Hopeville.

He'd put a slug between Bubba's eyes, turn Buchanan over to Major Tom Orly at the Ranger's station, then with his pardon finalized, McKenna would ride to Waco, claim his photography equipment, and travel around the world taking pictures.

Silently, he berated himself for the stupidity of kidnapping Audra.

He'd been too intent on using her as bait to draw out her brother and then carelessly allowed his emotions to get in the way.

****

The rough nudge galvanized McKenna into instant wakefulness. He eased his hand down and gripped his pistol. It took a moment for his eyes to adjust. He stared up at Audra. She wore the loose breeches and shirt that she detested. The slouch hat sat low over her brow.

"Wipe that ridiculous scowl off your face, and put your gun away." Audra nodded in mock seriousness. "Last night you said you'd swapped our horses for fresh mounts."

All business, she peered around at the filled stalls. "Which one is mine?"

In the dark hours of the morning, his mind sorted itself out into a decision. "I'm buying you a train ticket to however far it'll take you. There'll be enough left over to purchase stagecoach fare home."

"No." She stood with her hands on her hips.

McKenna lurched to his feet. Audra smelled of rain and rosewater, and the silken strands of her hair peeked from beneath her hat. The rain-spattered shirt outlined her breasts.

As he approached her, she slapped him, her hand lashing out to catch him full in the face, a resounding slap that twisted his head and left his ear ringing.

"What the hell was that for?"

"When you didn't come to the hotel last night, I thought something had happened to you." Audra's hand swept back and lashed out again. "You really are a bastard."

He caught her wrist and shoved her against the stall and looked down at her. Her face tilted up to him, the lips, as ever, inviting. He pulled her to him and lifted her to his kiss. She yielded, her arms encircling his neck. An ache building, growing within and striving to be unleashed, McKenna gasped and forced himself away. He knew where the next kiss would lead.

"I didn't mean for that to happen, Audra."

Her chest rose in rapid breaths. "It's all right." She touched his cheek, let her fingers trace the hard lines of his face, then abruptly turned and stooped to lift the saddle and horse blanket next to the stall. "Just so you know—I'll follow you. Might as well get used to it."

"The chestnut with the bald face." McKenna forced back a smile as he grabbed his own saddle. "He's yours."

Thunder rumbled outside the walls. McKenna slapped the rump of the buckskin gelding in the next stall, and while he saddled the horse, savored the taste of Audra's kiss on his lips—the kiss for tomorrow.

Chapter Ten

The distant peal of thunder drew a hunch to Audra's shoulders as she rode. Already she wore a canvas duster against the threat of a downpour. She cringed at the burst of thunder and the zigzag pattern of lightning. Urging her pony alongside McKenna's, she called out, "Why are we heading away from the stronghold?"

The storm drummed closer, and rain fell in fat drops. McKenna pointed to the northwest. "Buchanan took a slug in his kneecap. He'll need a sawbones, and the closest one is in Villa Carsiana."

"How much farther?" The thought of what lay ahead sent a chill through her.

He leaned closer to Audra to make himself heard. "Over the next rise."

****

Past noon, Audra followed McKenna. They rode right down the middle of the muddy street. A dog raced out, barking and nipping at the hind legs of Audra's gelding. An old man shouted and tossed a rock at the mutt, causing the animal to slink away.

"*¿Amigo, es Buchanan en el bar?*" McKenna inquired, asking if the outlaw was in the saloon.

A look of apprehension filled the old man's face as he glanced about. He lifted his arm and pointed toward a lone adobe building at the end of the street. "*No, señor. Él està en la casa del doctor.*"

When McKenna started to translate, Audra said, "I understood."

She asked the old man, "What about his son? Is he at the doctor's, too?"

The old Mexican seemed to inwardly cringe, and in broken English said, "The kid, him more crazy than all times before." He made the sign of the cross. "*Vaya con Dios.*" And he hastened away.

Audra turned frightened eyes toward McKenna and whispered, "Go with God."

McKenna turned his horse in front of a shabby adobe building. "It's the next best thing to a hotel." They dismounted and Audra followed him inside. McKenna made arrangements for a room and a meal. Once behind closed doors, Audra whirled about. "I'm going with you."

The biting grip of his hands on her arms brought a slight moan. He shook her as if she were a rag doll. "Get it through your thick skull, Audra. Bubba Buchanan is dangerous. You heard what the old man said."

McKenna didn't miss the defiance in her eyes, the steel in her voice. "You wanted to use me as bait…" Concern brought a quick change to her face. "If he is my brother, please…don't kill him."

McKenna released her. His black eyes made no change. "Forgive me for what I'm about to do, Audra."

In a flash, he lifted his fist and landed a right cross to her chin, then caught her in his arms as she sagged to the floor. "You'll hate me when you come to, but at least one of us will be alive." And he laid her gently on the bed.

Audra reminded him of a sleeping child. In that instant, he knew a life without her would never be complete. He puzzled about that for a moment. After kissing her, he pulled the big iron Colt from his holster and slammed two empty chambers with .45 caliber slugs. Spinning the cylinder, he pointed the revolver, sighted down the barrel, and then holstering the weapon, retied the two dangling leather thongs securing the holster to his thigh.

Long strides propelled McKenna toward the doctor's house. Not bothering to knock, he pushed open the slatted door, the .45 in his hand.

He found the doctor sprawled in a chair, an empty bottle in his hand. Snores filled the room.

Lying on a narrow cot, Pete Buchanan propped up on his elbows. "McKenna, been a long time, friend."

McKenna recognized murder in the outlaw's eyes. "Hands where I can see 'em, Pete." McKenna flicked back the sheet, grabbed the revolver, and stuck it in his belt.

Buchanan's voice beat against him. "Never did set right with me and the fellers the way Bubba shot you. Don't hold much with back shooters."

McKenna's mouth tightened. "Heard that in your old age you were gettin' afraid of the kid."

There was a depraved expression on the outlaw's face. "Whadda you want, McKenna—to stand there jawin' me to death?"

"Huh-uh." He smiled. "It's very simple. After I rid society of that braying, killer jackass you claim as son, I'm turning you over to the Texas Rangers."

"Never figured you'd turn yellow-dog lawman." Buchanan scrubbed a calloused hand over his beard-stubbled chin. "'Tween you and me, if'n I could get outta this bed, I'd put a bullet in the kid. He's rogue...evil as they come and gettin' worse every day. The day I found him, shoulda let 'im die of snake bite when he was a young'un."

"You would've done society a favor." McKenna gandered at the outlaw's swollen leg, then turned on his heel toward the door. "Reckon you ain't going anywhere with that busted knee."

****

Audra didn't know whether to be glad or sorry. She recognized him the moment he pushed through the batwing saloon doors and stepped into the street.

He was young, with a handsome, willful face dominated by a red and pouting mouth. But he was big, too—hulky, wide shoulders, and muscular arms straining at his shirt. And he wore two Colts on a single belt cinched around his lean waist, the holsters tied down in the manner of a gunfighter.

The rain had stopped, and the hot, humid air wavered heavily around her. Bubba Buchanan's mouth made a long and bitter curve against his taut tanned face. Audra's breath came in quick, sharp bursts.

"Andrew Tadlock...Andy. It's me, your twin sister, Audra." She snatched the hat from her head, revealing the shock of white hair.

The hard-eyed man stopped in his tracks and stared at her. Desperately, she spoke to him. "We had a farm on the bayous of South Carolina. You liked to swim and fish. You were ten years old the last time I saw you—"

She watched the direction of his eyes and knew her shirt revealed more than it should. "Don't know nothing 'bout no sister or farm, but you sure are a looker, *señorita.*" The southern drawl caused him to exaggerate when he said the word *señorita.*

He lifted the whiskey bottle to his mouth and swigged deep, then drew a hand across his mouth. There was an ugly dissenting manner about him as he swaggered toward her.

Her heart skittered and the words tumbled. "Andy, please. You must remember something about me. I'm your sister, your twin. Our mother's name was Roseanne. Papa's was John. We were born on Christmas Eve, nearly twenty years ago. For my ninth birthday, Papa gave me a puppy, and you...and you—" The memory of what he'd done to the little spotted dog was too painful, and she couldn't continue.

Bubba reached out and seized Audra by her arms. His face was blade-like, inset with the ice-blue eyes that glittered with a kind of insanity.

He'd moved like a big cat set for a kill. McKenna was right. Bubba's laughter reminded her of a braying donkey. For an instant, she was frozen in astonishment. He gave her a jeering smile.

McKenna's voice rang out. "Audra, back away."

Bubba's hands tightened, and with a steely grip, he pinned her against his chest. "Reckon you don't die easy, huh, McKenna."

"She doesn't mean you any harm, Bubba. Let 'er go."

Audra felt helpless. What could she do to make anything different? Nothing. She had no weapon, and while she desperately wanted to help her brother, she had no desire to let him kill McKenna.

****

McKenna met Bubba's eyes. What he read sent a faint chill down his spine. The boy's eyes reflected no soul. "This is between you and me, Bubba. I've got an old score to settle. 'Course, a back-shooter like you is the kind of coward that has to hide behind a woman."

Bubba snickered and hee-hawed but kept a tight grip on Audra. "I don't like it when people call me coward."

"Why don't you do something about it...*coward*?" McKenna hoped his goading would cause the lunatic to push Audra aside and draw his gun.

A rifle hammer clicked...a vague movement shifted at one side. McKenna cut his eyes away from Audra and Bubba.

A shot, followed immediately by another shot, blasted out in deafening twin explosions. Pete Buchanan hobbled forward, a Winchester to his shoulder.

McKenna jerked up his Colt, fired with sights on Pete Buchanan's chest, and saw the big man spin around and plunge face down in the dirt.

McKenna ran forward and reached Audra as she got unsteadily to her feet, blood soaking her shirt and dribbling down her sleeve.

He made her sit down while he shucked off his coat and ripped a strip from his shirt. No more than a flesh wound where the bullet had passed through her brother and grazed her collarbone. McKenna bound her shoulder tightly to stop the bleeding.

****

Audra felt her brother's body drive against her and then, with a gagging sigh, drop to his knees and topple sideways. She skittered to reach him.

Bubba lifted a hand and touched her face, his smile softened his features, and the eyes, once clouded with insanity, cleared. "I'm sorry about killing your puppy, Sissy."

"Oh, Andy, you know me." She cradled his head in her lap and ran her hands through his hair. "We searched for days. Why didn't you come home?"

"Couldn't. Got moccasin bit." Her brother coughed. Death rattled in his chest. "'Sides, made me mad when Papa said he was going to tan my hide for wringin' the neck of Mama's prized egg layer." He looked up at Audra, and as a cloud darkened the sun, the expression in his eyes changed. "I like killin' things." He reached up and gripped her throat.

And then he laughed that same braying sound, coughed bloody sputum, and the fire in his eyes died.

Struggling to her feet, she was engulfed in McKenna's arms. She held him tightly, fighting back the hysteria that made her want to scream.

Chapter Eleven

A week later, McKenna retold his story from the witness box in San Antonio. "Pete Buchanan himself admitted Bubba was a stone-cold killer. Even Fargo Wilson said Pete had gotten afraid of the boy. One thing certain, when Pete put two Winchester slugs dead center in the kid's back, it was no accident."

Major Tom Orly said, "And then what happened?"

McKenna shrugged. "There wasn't any blood lost between us, so I thought Pete was gunning for me. I drew my Colt and planted two .45s in his chest."

Orly said, "So it was self-defense?"

"That's about the size of it." McKenna stepped down, and when Audra was called to testify, he assisted her to the chair.

****

Audra touched the bandage where the same bullet that had killed her brother had also grazed her collarbone. She glanced past Major Orly to McKenna. The heat of the room seemed to close in on her. McKenna's smile and wink did little to calm her nerves. She reflected fleetingly on all the changes in her life.

She smiled stiffly when Major Orly spoke her name.

"Miss Tadlock, we all regret the misfortunes under which you found your twin brother. I'm certain it's worked an unnecessary hardship on your emotions."

The Texas Ranger cleared his throat.

The way he crossed his arms over his chest and squinted, as if scrutinizing her, made Audra uncomfortable. She felt her face flush and didn't know if it was from the heat or for fear of the questions he would ask. "Yes, Major Orly, to discover that after all these years of thinking my brother dead, and then...and then finding him alive, but—" She couldn't find the words to express the sorrow that her brother was an *evil killer*. Instead, she glanced down and fidgeted with the pleats in her skirt.

"It's not my intent to add to your stress, Miss Tadlock. I do, however, have one more question." Major Orly offered a brief glance toward McKenna.

She too looked at McKenna and watched his handsome features stiffen. She knew the question the Texas Ranger was about to ask and also knew McKenna's fate lay in her answer.

****

McKenna cursed himself inwardly for bringing Audra to this. He stared at her, knowing the things he wished to say had all been left unsaid.

Her eyes looked like two huge bruises against her bleached expression. The barest of smiles flickered across her lips. He hadn't realized how seeing her seated in the witness box, her expression filled with remorse, would affect him.

He hadn't thought he would ever care about anyone again, especially a girl whose brother had tried to kill him. But he did care, and the pain of it hit him like a mule's kick to the chest.

I'm losing her just when I've found her—I've never even told her how much she matters to me. I've never told her I love her.

Major Orly's booming voice filled the room and brought McKenna out of his reverie. "Miss Tadlock, did McKenna Smith take you as hostage and use you as bait to lure out the outlaw known as Bubba Buchanan for the purpose of seeking retribution?"

For an instant, an overpowering feeling of futility washed over McKenna. He felt it rise through his body like a tide.

It took a moment for his stunned mind to grasp the full meaning of Audra's simple statement. She circumvented further questioning with her answer.

"No, Major Orly. Mr. Smith did not use me as a hostage. And now if that is all, my arm aches, and I am very tired."

****

Twenty minutes later, McKenna and Audra sat in the Texas Ranger's office. He was exhausted, his nerves drawn tightly. Was it over—was he a free man?

If only he could know what Audra was thinking. There were tears in her eyes.

Major Orly glanced from Audra to McKenna. "I haven't been a Ranger for nigh on twenty years without knowing something's fishy when I smell it, McKenna, but I ain't about to muddy the waters to find out." He reached across the desk to hand McKenna an envelope. "With Pete and Bubba Buchanan dead and most of the gang sitting in prison, the governor willingly concedes you've held up your end of the bargain."

Orly stood. "That there document is your full pardon."

McKenna didn't answer immediately. He shook hands with the Ranger, then turned to Audra and kissed her tear-wet cheeks. What he read in her eyes tripped his heart.

Chapter Twelve

Audra stood at the ship's railing, gazing out over the ocean. She remembered the emotional day when she and McKenna had stepped down from the stagecoach in Hopeville and surprised her aunt. She was even more surprised to learn that in her absence Aunt Sophie had married Sheriff Horace Rooks and seemed truly happy.

Audra had then packed all her worldly belongings in a sturdy chest, ready to follow McKenna to the ends of the earth. She vaguely remembered leaving Major Orly's office in San Antonio and McKenna hustling her over to the Justice of the Peace office.

She had stood quietly, as if in a dream, and listened as the voice of the justice slowly drifted away. She knew only that she was beside McKenna Smith, the man she loved and with whom she wished to spend her life, and they were binding their love in the most cherished way of all.

She recalled speaking the words, "I do," and had heard McKenna say them, too. Then his trembling hand had slipped a gold band onto her finger, and McKenna's mouth gently closed on her own. The thing that wasn't vague about her wedding day was the depth of love she held for her new husband.

That evening he had taken her to the finest dress shops in San Antonio and outfitted her with several new dresses and shoes and hats. After satisfying himself she had everything she could possibly need, he went on to order several new sets of clothing for himself.

They had dined in the finest restaurant, with champagne, and McKenna had carried her over the threshold of their hotel room.

So deep was she in her thoughts she didn't hear him approach. He wrapped his arms around her from behind. "Have I told you lately how much I love you?"

She smiled as she turned against his chest. "Hmm, not since breakfast." She shivered against him.

"Cold?"

"Huh-uh. Warm with desire." She didn't feel the damp sea air's chill as she stood on tiptoe to press her lips against her husband's.

These past four weeks had been the happiest of her life. McKenna had sold his guns and replaced them with new and modern camera equipment.

She'd never thought to ask him how he'd had enough money to purchase tickets for an extended tour of Europe. He said he'd seen his fill of the West for a while. He told of the books he'd read about London and Paris and of his desire to photograph the people and lands of China and Africa. Caught up in the fever of his excitement, she'd never questioned how they could afford such an adventure.

Now his handsome face was ever so close to her own, an amused twinkle in his eyes. A smile played upon his lips. Her heart thumped wildly. She pulled his head down. "Kiss me, McKenna."

"You're a wanton wench, wife." He lifted her into his arms and, with long, swift strides, carried her to their cabin.

After he'd secured the door, she slipped from her

gown and layers of crinolines and slid beneath the bed's coverlet.

"We'll make the world our home, Mrs. McKenna Smith."

"Mrs. McKenna Smith...I like the sound of that." She propped on one elbow and watched him shed his clothes. "I can't believe how happy I am."

Nestling next to her, he buried his head against her tightly bound breasts. "And I would feel happier if there were no fabric to bar me from you."

"Then what are you waiting for, husband? Get rid of the blasted thing."

His mouth curled into a rakish grin. McKenna's eyes remained steady as he unbound the cloth. His quiet strength and warm smile filled her. He brushed his lips against hers, then kissed the corners of her mouth. Audra trembled under the feathery touch.

A delicious torrent of love surged through her, and she knew that all her days and nights would be filled with McKenna. Life wouldn't be perfect. She didn't know if he could earn enough money selling his photographs for them to live on, but she would spend the rest of her life with him. *Through thick and thin, through sickness and sorrow, 'til death us do so part.* She meant every word of her vow.

"I'm not sure how all this happened. I just know that it's wonderful." She released a contented sigh as she moved within the radius of his arms.

"I kidnapped you, remember?" He kissed her hard.

"Yes, and I disliked you immensely. I shot you, *remember*?" Her lips pinched together as she played the game of cat-and-mouse.

"Ah, so you did shoot me on purpose? And here all

this time I thought you really meant to kill that rattler."

Her eyes widened. "Oh, you think me a violent woman?"

He wrapped her tightly in his arms and kissed her. "I think you a woman filled with enormous passion."

With all her pent-up longings, Audra protested when he pulled away. She marveled at the chiseled sculpture of his muscled back, but winced at the scars that puckered the skin where he'd been shot. She shuddered and shoved away the thought of her brother.

McKenna walked naked to the sea chest and bent over to open the trunk. "I have something for you."

She gave a disdainful sniff. "At the moment, you are all I want."

While admiring every luscious inch of his body, she unconsciously thumbed the gold band around her finger. Her body hummed with desire while she watched him.

He rummaged beneath the stacks of his neatly packed clothing and removed a brown envelope, then came to sit on the edge of the narrow bed next to Audra. Emotion rippled his voice. "I never gave you a proper wedding present."

She looked at the envelope in her hand, questions in her eyes. "What is it?"

"You'll never know if you don't open it."

Her curiosity piqued, she sat up and carefully slid her thumbnail under the envelope's sealed flap and drew out its contents.

Surprise and delight gleamed in her eyes. "I don't believe it! How…?" Her voice choked with emotion, she whispered, "But how did you…?" Her eyes scanned the document that titled her to full ownership of her childhood homestead on Bayou George in South Carolina.

Sitting beside her, he took the document and slipped it back inside the envelope. "*How* doesn't matter. The only thing that matters, Mrs. Smith, is *now*, our waiting bed, a beautiful woman, and the man who loves her."

How strange life was, she thought, remembering all the times she had lamented to her aunt, desiring to travel and yet certain that she would perish from boredom.

"Penny for your thoughts, wife." McKenna smoothed his hand over her breasts and drew her near.

She knew his arms were her destiny. When she gazed up at him, his eyes were soft and warm. And mirrored in the depths of his gaze she saw where she wanted to be for all of her life.

"I'm thinking how much I want you to make love to me, husband."

As McKenna moved against her, his lean body rocking in rhythm as timeless as man and woman, she felt the quickening of her pulses, the shuddering reaction of her body to his pounding beat. A slight tremor rocked her, which grew into a towering tide that washed over her in wave after wave of aching pleasure. She didn't even realize she'd cried out or that she was digging her fingers into his back. There was only that sweeping gale of the senses that carried her along in a breathless rush.

Then McKenna groaned, and she could feel his pulse race before his body relaxed against hers. Reality came slowly back, and Audra smiled in contentment. When he rolled away from her, she propped on an elbow. With the other hand, she toyed with the dark hairs on his chest.

He clasped her hand and brought it to his mouth to kiss her fingers. "Something's troubling you, Audra. I can read it in your eyes."

Her mouth softened. "Are we rich? I mean, how can we afford all the adventures you speak of?"

Scooting up to a sitting position, he lifted Audra onto his lap so she straddled him. He let out a long breath. "The reward money for Pete Buchanan and his gang was substantial."

Audra's face crumpled into a disappointed frown, and she tried to pull away. He held tight to her arms. "I had Major Orly donate half the reward money on Bubba to an orphanage. The rest I sent to your aunt. She's made a lot of sacrifices in her lifetime to protect and raise you."

With infinite tenderness, Audra cupped McKenna's face in her hands. She pressed her lips against his and whispered, "Have I told you how much I love you?"

And she knew that no truer words had ever been spoken.

Loretta C. Rogers

A word about the author...

Aside from the fact she gets to be her own boss and go to work in her pjs, Loretta C. Rogers enjoys writing because she gets to live vicariously through her characters that are clever and fearless, but in real life Loretta is afraid of snakes and heights. Let's face it: she wouldn't last five minutes in one of her books. The thing she appreciates most is when readers accuse her of keeping them up all night turning the pages of one of her novels. She also loves that she gets paid to make stuff up.

Loretta has no hobbies because writing is all-consuming and takes a lot out of her. A multi-genre author, her books are available in print, ebook, and audio books. You can contact her at:

www.lorettacrogersnovels.com

~*~

Other titles
available from The Wild Rose Press, Inc.

Taming the Lyon
Murder in the Mist
Shadowed Reunion
Cloud Woman's Spirit
Lady Adel's Captain
The Witching Moon
Forbidden Son
Bannon's Brides
McKenna's Woman
Isabelle and the Outlaw

Thank you for purchasing
this publication of The Wild Rose Press, Inc.

If you enjoyed the story, we would appreciate your
letting others know by leaving a review.

For other wonderful stories,
please visit our on-line bookstore at
www.thewildrosepress.com.

For questions or more information
contact us at
info@thewildrosepress.com.

The Wild Rose Press, Inc.
www.thewildrosepress.com

Stay current with The Wild Rose Press, Inc.

Like us on Facebook

https://www.facebook.com/TheWildRosePress

And Follow us on Twitter
https://twitter.com/WildRosePress